BABY FIGHTS

Robert Essig

Infected Voices Publishing

Copyright © 2023 by Robert Essig

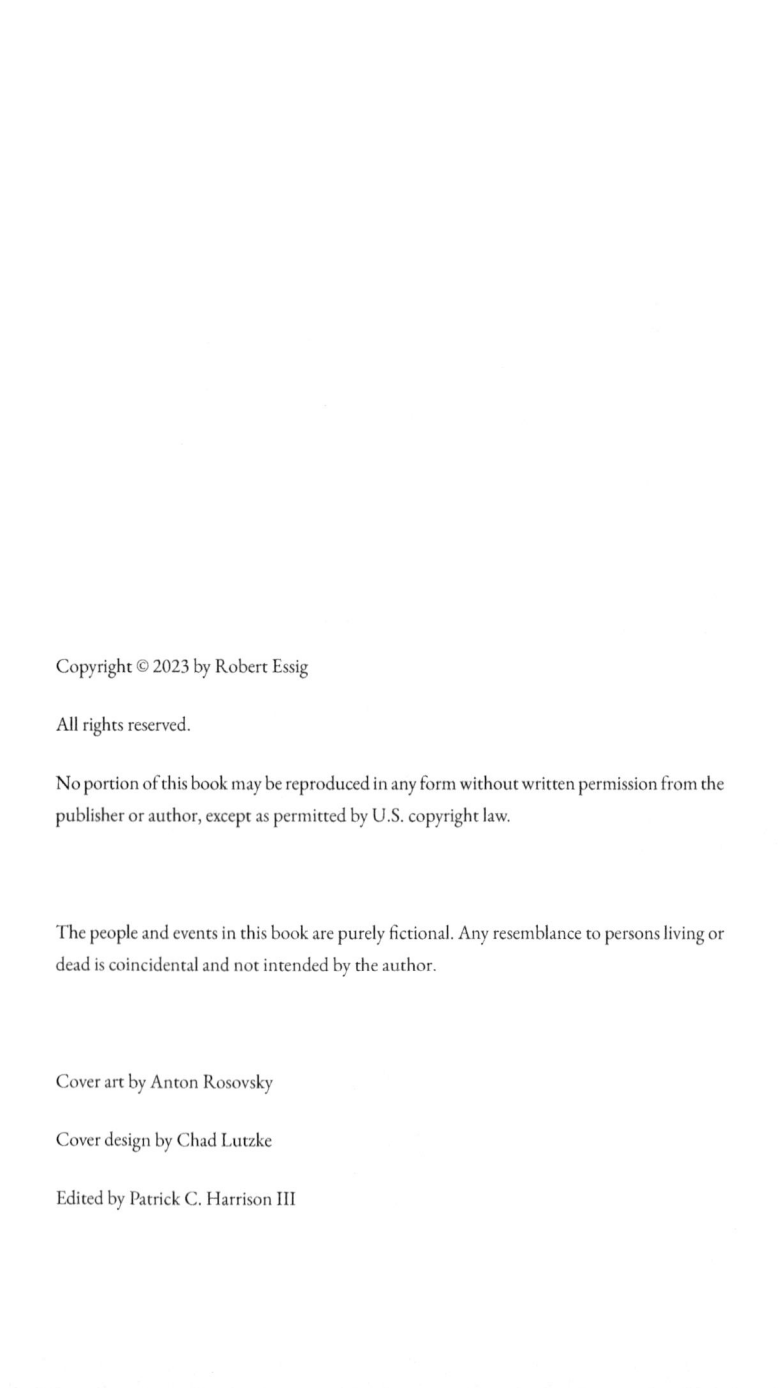

All rights reserved.

No portion of this book may be reproduced in any form without written permission from the publisher or author, except as permitted by U.S. copyright law.

The people and events in this book are purely fictional. Any resemblance to persons living or dead is coincidental and not intended by the author.

Cover art by Anton Rosovsky

Cover design by Chad Lutzke

Edited by Patrick C. Harrison III

WARNING

This book is every bit as fucked up as the title suggests. You have been warned. For the sickos out there, proceed and enjoy.

Prologue

It all started with cockfights. No, not what you're thinking, not with roosters. With cocks. Dicks. Rods. Francis "Ducky" Winchester started it. He was nicknamed Ducky as a kid because his lips sort of looked like duck lips the way they curled outward. His parents thought it was funny and cute, but probably didn't think, at the time, the name would stick. His lips looked normal now, but the moniker stuck. Everyone had always called him Ducky.

Anyway, the cockfights started when Ducky was maybe eleven or twelve. He and his friends were starting to get hard-ons for no reason at all. Sometimes it was because of a scene in a movie they were watching or maybe while they perused porn sites on the Internet, but really they'd just get hard sometimes. It happened. So, of course, they started grabbing their little rods and declaring sword fights, Ducky being the primary instigator.

The way things turned out, it was no wonder Ducky would go on to start Baby Fights. See, the boys would get going, swatting at one another like they were brandishing light sabers, making obnoxious *vroom vroom* noises to mimic *Star Wars*. Ducky was only getting harder while they did this. He never thought of the homoerotic implications of it all. They were just kids having fun with their God given erections, but he took it a step further. He was a bit more endowed than his friends, so he could get a good grip at the base. He'd swing that cock like a baseball bat, really putting force into it. He and his friends Joel and Marc were giggling and laughing one night in his room after Ducky's parents were asleep (they couldn't hear him anyway, their room being on the other side of the damn mini mansion they lived in). Ducky got a look in his eyes. He went after Joel first, swatting at Joel's pecker with this thing he was squeezing tight, filled with blood like a fleshy mallet. The whack hurt Joel, his smile replaced with anger.

"Hey, what'd you do that for?" Joel said.

Ducky responded by using his cock-hammer to whack Joel again, even harder. At this point, Joel's erection was becoming flaccid, but he was left with a red mark on his penis, compliments of Ducky's efforts.

It was then that Ducky turned to Marc. Ducky let go of his erection, and it just bobbed there, all dark and engorged. He was enjoying this way too much.

Mark shook his head. "Don't do that to me," he said, but he was still erect. Somehow the smackdown Ducky gave Joel didn't faze Marc, at least not his groin. He had one of those stubborn hard-ons, the ones that come out of nowhere and stick around for a while, and always just before being called to the front of class or when he had to stand in line or something.

Ducky grabbed his dick like a weapon. The pressure he put on the thing when he gripped it made the head swell even more, shining glossy against the light in the room. He kind of hunched over like some barbarian preparing for battle, and then he moved forward. Marc tried to remove himself from the situation, but Ducky used his free hand and grabbed Marc by the shoulder, swinging his body around so they were facing each other. Ducky used this opportunity to swat at Marc's erection with his own. He used it like a fucking weapon, like it wasn't even attached to his body. He swung it hard and precise. Ended up getting two good shots in before Marc collapsed onto the ground crying and yelling like a pussy. Marc was never the same. From that day on there was a bend in his erection, which turned out to be a happy accident, as years later girls would claim that, despite it looking bizarre, the kink in his hard cock felt great during sex.

That was the beginning. The seed for Baby Fights had been sowed.

One

At three o'clock on an August afternoon Madison Holzer cursed the sun for at least the twelfth time that day as she struggled with the car seat in the Wal-Mart parking lot at the end of Los Cochas Road in El Cajon, an eastern community of San Diego. El Cajon translated to The Box, but Madison figured they should have called it The Pit. It was a giant valley that collected stagnant hot air like an oven, broiling the residents this time of year. The whole 76 and sunny bullshit people associate with San Diego was only relevant to the wealthy folks who lived in the beach communities, or in the north county.

As Madison finagled with the straps of the car seat, her baby boy Hunter got himself all worked up and started crying, which soon turned to full-on braying, as if he was working out his lungs. Madison wondered just how safe the car seat really was. There were specs they had to meet, and parents were urged not to use secondhand car seats. She couldn't even take Hunter home from the hospital without putting him into an approved car seat, and proving that she could get

BABY FIGHTS

him secured, which had been a nightmare. Madison was lucky to have her mother there, considering the sperm donor had skipped out just about as quick as he heard the news that he was going to be a father.

Sweat ran down her temples as she became more frustrated. Yeah, this thing was safe all right. It would safely carry the baby into the flames were she to find herself in a fiery wreck while Madison struggled with the godforsaken straps.

Finally she got the baby out. It wasn't always that difficult, but it was hot and Madison had been running around all day, and the damn car seat got the better of her. Just when she'd gotten used to the little newborn car seat, she had to upgrade to this baby-to-toddler seat, which came with a whole new set of instructions and pitfalls to stress parents to the max. Baby in one arm, purse slung over the other shoulder, Madison was ready to brave the hoards at Wal-Mart, and she knew it would be bad, considering she had to park at the back of the lot. Had she not desperately needed milk and diapers, she would have let it wait until Monday.

After using a wet wipe on just about any surface of the cart the baby could grasp onto, shifting to keep her overstuffed purse from sliding down her arm, and holding Hunter tight, she slid him into the little child seat, his pudgy legs slipping through the openings. She placed her purse within the main part of the cart. Hunter looked into her eyes as she pushed the cart forward, the tiny wheels rumbling loudly on the asphalt, the cart itself rattling so hard Hunter's whole body quivered. But he didn't seem to mind. As he looked into his mother's eyes he smiled, as if he enjoyed the sensation.

Madison remembered when that top foldout area in the cart had been used for soft or delicate items like bread and eggs, to be sure they didn't get crushed by the heavier groceries she would place in the main part of the cart. Now, were she to put a loaf of bread beside Hunter, he would throw it out or use it like a stress reliever, squishing the softness with his eager hands. Things that were cute at first, but grated on her nerves these days.

On days such as this one, Madison wished more than ever that she had someone at home to watch Hunter so she could have just a little bit of alone time. Even if that alone time was spent shopping for groceries, it would give her a break. A desperately needed break. Madison was finding out the hard way that there was no time off for good behavior in adulthood. Especially for a single mother whose sperm donor vanished like a master magician.

By the time Madison made it into the Wal-Mart, she was already exhausted. She was beginning to think the parking stalls in the front that were reserved for pregnant women should be for mothers with young children as well. But she figured she needed the exercise. Getting rid of the extra pregnancy weight had not been as easy as some women made it out to be on social media. How the hell those bitches found the time to work out after dealing with a baby all day, not to mention nighttime feedings, was beyond her. On top of the struggle to get her body back, she hadn't been eating quite as well as she'd like. When Madison was pregnant she ate pretty much whatever she wanted. As it turned out, that was a hard habit to break, as evidenced when she walked through the aisles choosing flavor over health when it came to snacks and dinner prep.

As she was choosing the softest loaf of fresh baked $1.49 French bread (*wasn't this just .99 cents last week?*), Madison noticed a young couple with a baby. The woman was maybe four years younger than her. The man, presumably her husband, was helping as they navigated the store. It wasn't that Madison singled out couples such as this one, but that she couldn't help but see them all around her, every day. It was like buying a new car and suddenly seeing that same model everywhere. They were always there, but when they held no significance, they just sort of remained in the background.

Madison envied those couples. It took her a long time to accept that. Even if Hunter had a father who was in the picture, even if they were separated, at least that would be something. Raising him all by herself had been, so far, an uphill battle. She loved Hunter more than anything, but it was hard not to feel like he completely took over her life. Those few fleeting times she could depend on her mother to watch him, times she thought that maybe she could go out to a club with friends like she used to do, or maybe have a girls' night, all Madison wanted was a night of undisturbed sleep.

She had no social life to speak of. Hardly enough time for her friends. Mostly she went on the occasional lunch meeting to catch up, but most of her friends were finishing college, living life. They valued career over the traditional idea of a woman being a baby factory in that illusion of domestic bliss so many ads in the 50s and 60s boasted about. Madison had once been just like them. Until Trevor Gifford Ryan came into her life, the son of a bitch.

When they first met she'd thought she found The One. He was handsome, tall, put together, and came from good stock, which was a nice way to say he came from money. Trevor knew how to talk to a woman. Knew exactly what to say to make Madison feel wanted, to feel loved, to feel pined for. That was everything she could have asked for. He was a true romantic. Like something out of a fucking

Hallmark movie. She should have known he was too good to be true, just stringing her along for the sex. She'd fallen so hard for him that she forgot about all the precaution she'd taken with men. Madison wasn't on the pill, so she had always made sure her sexual partners used condoms, but she became lax with Trevor. That was mostly due to his insistence that it just didn't feel as good with the condom on, and that was true. He was so persuasive, but not in a pushy sort of way, at least at the time she hadn't thought so. He told her he would pull out. Everything would be okay. He even hinted at marriage, telling her that once they were married they could think about starting a family, then they would never have to use those stupid condoms again.

And so Trevor pulled out. Right up until he didn't. And Madison, foolishly fallen for the prick, allowed him to come inside. Their lovemaking was epic, and she had to admit that she found it hard to climax with those damn condoms on. When they were coming together, the last thing she wanted was for him to pull out. It was selfish on both their parts, and here, nearly a year later, was the result. Hunter Holzer.

Trevor left days after Madison told him he was going to be a father. Their last text messages were heated. She'd been begging him to respond. He'd given her the silent treatment. She'd even gone to his house, but no one was there. He'd moved that quickly, as if becoming a father was a death sentence. The last text she sent him said: *If u don't talk to me I'll abort your baby*. To which Trevor responded: *Do it. I dare you.*

And because of that, she kept the baby.

Tracking Trevor down for child support had been, at this point, futile. Seemed that Trevor wasn't even his real name. And if it was, he'd somehow changed it. Madison couldn't imagine someone going through such measures to avoid the responsibilities of fatherhood. Sure, deadbeat men flee the babies they make, and often they make them with a multitude of partners, but how many of those assholes drop off the face of the planet?

Madison caught a glimpse of herself in one of those long mirrors in the clothing aisle. It was a slimming mirror designed to make women look good. Despite the trials and tribulations of being a single mother, she tried to keep herself buttoned up and put together. She'd scaled down her makeup to something that was more highlights than going clubbing, but she never left the house without it. She wore clothes that accentuated her body and hid the baby fat she couldn't seem to get rid of. But underneath it all she saw a tired woman. Especially in the eyes. Madison wondered if everyone else saw that.

Hunter cooed, drawing her attention away from the mirror. He garbled out a series of syllables, as if trying to speak words. Looking into his light brown eyes flaked with gold, Madison smiled, and he smiled back. Were she to look into the mirror at that moment and see the smile, she might not even see the haunted eyes staring back.

She pushed the cart forward, passing the clothing section (something it used to take a load of will power to do, even in a place like Wal-Mart), and headed for the aisle with floor to ceiling diapers.

Finally, Hunter became agitated and Madison could see that he was about to get into one of his crying fits. She dug her arm into her purse and rummaged around for a pacifier. There must have been five of them in there. Pulling one out, she made sure it didn't have any lint or purse debris on it, and stuck it in Hunter's mouth. He greedily accepted, and, for that moment at least, all was right in Madison's world. Making her way to the front of the store, she checked out her groceries, looking forward to getting home, getting Hunter down for a nap, and then taking a nap of her own.

But Madison didn't make it home that evening.

Two

THE RIGID CART RIDE back to Madison's car at the back of the parking lot seemed to soothe Hunter. His chubby cheeks jiggled as the cart vibrated from the uneven pavement, which managed to get a smile out of Madison. Hunter looked up at her, mouth agape, spittle beginning to drip off his bottom lip from the vibrations. Precious moments like these caused Madison to have no regrets. Fuck Trevor Gifford Ryan. He was the one missing out. He would never know who his son was, and she would make sure of that. He'd lost that privilege.

At her car, she left Hunter in the cart as she unloaded her groceries into the trunk. Madison had this fear that were she to put Hunter into the car first, she would mistakenly lock the doors with keys inside. Just thinking about leaving her baby in the car by mistake caused her to feel panicked. She'd heard that people left their children in cars on summer days, only to have them roast to death. It was awful to think about, but it happened all the time. Being a young mother of one, Madison couldn't imagine doing such a thing. She figured it must have been people with a great deal of stress. People preoccupied with work when they should perhaps slow things down. No matter how Madison tried to rationalize it, she couldn't understand accidentally leaving a child in a hot car.

Whenever she was at a low moment in this thing called single motherhood, she thought about the precautions she took when it came to Hunter, and she realized that though some of her thoughts went into very dark places, Hunter was the love of her life, and she would do anything to protect him.

The problem in that moment was that sometimes there was nothing a young mother could do to protect her baby, especially when two men came out of nowhere to snatch Hunter.

Madison saw the shadow creep around her face. She recoiled as the chloroform soaked rag was slammed across her mouth and nose, and held there tight. The last thing she saw was another man grab Hunter, pulling him from the cart, and then Madison lost consciousness.

Three

Ducky lived in the ritzy east San Diego neighborhood of Blossom Valley, where the houses were big, the yards spacious, and the rumors were that several actors, musicians, and sports stars owned homes there on the down low. Ducky knew for a fact that pop sensation Justin Dudar had a place in Blossom Valley. He also knew that Justin was into Baby Fights, something Ducky could hold over Justin if he needed to; not that he had much leverage. It wasn't like Baby Fights were legal. Ducky would be put in prison just as quick as Justin Dudar's career dive bombed were his fans to find out that he took pleasure in watching babies fight to the death.

Most of the people who enjoyed Baby Fights came from out of the neighborhood. Ducky liked it that way. If he were to get too many locals in on it, they would begin to look at him differently. Someone might slip and say something. It was too risky. This operation wasn't merely some lurid YouTube video-esque level sickness, like paying homeless people to punch each other. This was serious stakes money, with human life lost, which was comical to Ducky, considering he was a top donor to pro-life groups in greater San Diego County. Had to get those write-offs. And hell, pro-life meant more fighting babies.

Ducky's house was situated up a drive off a dead end road. It wasn't a cul-de-sac, per se. Just a road that ended with a yellow traffic sign that said Dead End, stating the obvious. Kids liked to park their cars at the end of the street, smoke dope and make out. Ducky watched them with infrared binoculars. It was a voyeur thing. He liked to watch. He liked getting glimpses of tender young flesh, though it was often hard to see through the windows, especially when they got all steamed up, or the kids hot-boxed the car with marijuana smoke.

The house had been left to Ducky by his parents, along with quite a nice inheritance. It had taken years of watching Investigation Discovery and loads of documentaries on murder for him to plan the perfect crime. If the myriad of programs on Investigation Discovery taught Ducky anything, it was what people did wrong when they planned on killing someone, or especially when they murdered spontaneously. Always leaving too much evidence or staging a crime scene wrong. Always too elaborate or not well thought out. Always done on impulse or by people who couldn't plan a dinner party much less a murder.

Over the years, Ducky had taken a fancy to his father's hobby of piloting airplanes. Father owned his own, a top-of-the-line private plane that they used for quick jaunts up the coast or even to Las Vegas. Father loved that plane, and he loved the craft. For a man who had made his fortune in business, with hands as soft as leather, Father enjoyed tinkering on his plane more than anything. And Ducky did too. He learned a lot by watching Father. Enough that he knew exactly what to manipulate to cause the plane to fail in the air. The key was that it had to look like mechanical failure. Ducky couldn't put oil in the gas tank or some other numbskull move that would hint at sabotage.

And it worked. The plane went down somewhere in Riverside while his parents were on their way to a dinner party in Los Angeles. Ever the actor, Ducky grieved properly (something he picked up on those programs he watched), and in no time the estate and all of his parents' money was his, thanks to the living trust and him being an only child.

Privilege. Don't leave home without it.

Standing before the picture window in the master suite, looking out over the front driveway, Ducky held tight his pistol. No matter how many times they'd done this, he couldn't shake the nerves until Ryan and Chance got back. If they were caught and they snitched, it would be no less than a swarm of police cars that showed up. In that event, Ducky would type in a command on his computer, releasing his manifesto and a complete ledger of attendees from his infamous Baby Fights, and then he would nestle the barrel of the gun under his chin, right in the soft spot beneath his tongue, and he'd blow his brains out the top of his head (and that's what would happen, because he kept hollow points in that particular pistol).

Over the past three years Ducky had envisioned a way to produce babies for these events, that way the risk of going out and snatching them would be eliminated, but he couldn't think of a way to do such a thing. With pregnancy taking nine months, plus conception, it just didn't make sense. He'd have to have a whole wing of the house sectioned off like a hospital with little rooms for each expecting mother, a doctor and nurse on staff, plus access to medical equipment and the proper care so the mothers had healthy pregnancies. It was a lot to comprehend, but sometimes Ducky thought he could pull it off if he tried. The women would have to be in different stages of pregnancy, and then the babies would have to be raised in some sort of nursery by a small team of nannies before they were at that perfect age for Baby Fights.

Ducky shook his head. Thinking about that kind of operation made his brain hurt. That was his ultimate goal, but it just seemed too risky. It was hard enough to trust Ryan and Chase, much less an in-home doctor, nurse, and team of nannies. They'd all have to be the right kind of freak to participate in something so morally bankrupt. It went against the fabric of human nature to raise babies for fighting.

When the Chrysler 300 pulled up the drive, Ducky took a breath. He placed the pistol back into the top drawer of his bureau. The gun had one hollow point in it, always loaded in the chamber. Always ready for a quick escape.

By the time Ducky got into the garage, the large door was closing. The Chrysler idled, its engine ticking. Ducky stood there, not able to see much inside of the car, hoping that everything went well and they had a new contestant to add to their corral.

Ryan got out of the driver's side, his face chiseled and smooth and so much like a college yuppie it was sickening, right down to his sweater and tapered jeans. His hair was perfect, as if frozen in place. His cologne greeted Ducky before he did, which was customary for Ryan. If you got too close or, god forbid, hugged the guy, you were done for the day. You couldn't get the smell of him off you. He gave Ducky a curt nod that said more than words. Ducky returned the gesture.

The passenger side door opened, and out came Chance. He was dressed similarly, though he sported a well-manicured hipster beard that hid his face from the world, cloaking him in a mask of secrecy. His trademark unlit cigarette dangled from the bush on his face. He was impossible to read, and he seemed to like it that way. He offered a curt nod, to which Ducky reciprocated.

Everything had gone well.

Chance opened the passenger side rear door, as Ryan did the same on the driver's side. Ducky felt a surge of excitement as they revealed their score. It was akin to the endorphin rush sex and drugs offered, only stronger. Junkies enjoyed the rush of meeting with their dealer almost as much as putting the junk into their veins, and these two goons were about to deal up something good.

Ryan pulled out a healthy baby boy. The child had a cherub face and a look of bemusement. There was some cartoon character on his shirt that Ducky didn't recognize. The baby was quite docile after all he had been through. Ryan approached Ducky, holding out the baby like an offering.

"He looks good," Ducky said.

Ryan nodded. "Doesn't get any easier, but no one saw us. We got Mom back there too. We drugged her up so she wouldn't start anything."

"Of course. You'd have been foolish to do it any other way." Putting his arms out, Ducky gestured for Ryan to hand over the baby. "You help Chance."

Ryan handed over the baby and then assisted Chance with the woman. She was so drugged up she couldn't stand, but she was conscious, her eyes opening just a slit, as if trying to avoid the florescent lights in the garage. It was the drug, whatever Ryan and Chance put in her veins. Ducky didn't ask. He didn't care, so long as she was unconscious or close to that.

Ducky went into the house, followed by Ryan and Chance, who carried the woman, her feet dragging along the floor. Once inside, the baby started fussing.

"I guess he doesn't like your décor," Ryan said.

Ducky held the baby out, tilted his head and pursed his lips, which was the only time they twisted up into the duckbill look that was his namesake. "I think he's hungry. Get momma on the couch."

The woman was carried to one of the couches and sloughed onto it like a drunk co-ed after a wild night at the clubs.

"Get her shirt off," Ducky said. He smiled. "Let's see those milkers."

Chance grabbed the woman's shirt and pulled it over her head, wiggling it around to bypass her slack arms. Ryan reached around and unclasped her bra. Up close, he looked into her listless eyes, and for just a second, a fleeting moment, her eyes widened with recognition, and then was lost to the ethers of her drugged-up mind. He pulled the bra away and looked at her.

Ryan nodded. "Yeah, she's feeding him. Those titties are engorged. Get that baby over here."

Ducky brought the baby over, placing him on his splayed-out mother, the child's face near her right nipple. He was awkward with the child. Using an almost ridiculous amount of caution for a man who was intent on having this baby go to battle against other infants.

Chance said, "There's probably a certain way she holds him."

Ducky kind of shrugged. "Yeah, well, she can't exactly do that right now."

After several moments and failed attempts, the baby latched, bracing its legs to keep from falling off the couch.

Ducky smiled. "That was a good idea, bringing the mom like that. Some of the babies have been such a pain in the ass when they refuse formula." Ducky snickered. "You're looking at the milk bar, boys. She'll feed all the babies."

Chance tilted his head, eye squinting. "Will that work? Other babies will take to a different mother?"

Ducky looked sideways at Chance. He couldn't see the look of bemusement on his face due to the hipster beard, but he knew it was there. The beard caused Chance to look far more menacing than he really was. It was his defense mechanism, and it worked. People tended to leave him the fuck alone, even if some of the stupidest things came out of his mouth.

"Of course it will work," Ducky said. "Same species. Ever heard about a dog that takes in stray cats and feeds them. It happens in nature like that sometimes. Not even the same species, and yet the milk is good enough. Don't be such a fucking idiot, Chance."

Chance's eyes deepened. He pulled the unlit cigarette out of his mouth. His lips tightened behind his sandy beard. Ryan snickered, but if he had a wisecrack to say, he kept it to himself. Chance shot him a glance like icy daggers, but Ryan didn't even flinch, much less take that icy look to heart.

As the baby finished, his mother's head shifted and her eyes opened slightly, like someone waking to a room of overhead lights, trying to keep the brightness from searing into her retinas. She mumbled out a few incoherent words, and then her body went limp again.

"Hmm. She's already coming out of it," Ducky said. "Let's get her into a room. Somewhere near the nursery. There's a spare bedroom next to it, the one with dresser and TV mounted on the wall. Take all that shit out. Just leave the bed. Turn the doorknob around so we can lock it from the outside. We'll install a deadbolt later this week."

Chance and Ryan nodded, and then headed away to prepare the room.

Ducky pulled the baby from its mother's breast. The baby protested at first, but Ducky had always had a way with babies. He knew how to coo them, how to comfort them, just where to tickle them. This baby was putty in his hands, looking up into Ducky's smiling face like he was the very promise of a good binky and a soft crib to sleep in.

Momma was left sprawled out on the couch, milk leaking from her nipples.

Four

Ducky's dream of an underground Baby Fight empire had been slow to start, but was gaining traction with every main event. It was risky. So very risky. Ducky wasn't one who trusted easily. He had rules for those who found out about Baby Fights and wanted to secure a seat as a spectator. Kind of like when a dealer asks a new customer to do a bump before they exchange drugs and money.

The house Ducky inherited from his parents was huge, nestled into five acres, what Ducky liked to call a sprawling ranch, not that he'd ever actually *seen* a real ranch. This gave him privacy. The house itself was over four thousand square feet. Three stories. Six bedrooms and eight bathrooms. Most of the bedrooms had a bathroom to accompany them, much like individual master suites, however two of the bedrooms shared a Jack and Jill bathroom. Those two bedrooms became the nurseries.

There was a stairwell on either side of the house, both leading to the second floor. Only one stairwell lead to the master suite on top, consisting of the entire third level. Ducky had always liked that his parents had the house built like this. They'd been rich beyond belief. Not only did they work themselves to death for local tech companies, they'd been early investors in Qualcomm *and* Google. Now, all that was theirs belonged to Francis Winchester, better known as Ducky. He didn't have to work a day in his life, but his passion for baby fights was what he woke up for every day, even if he worked at a loss, which he certainly didn't. His parents' money was invested wisely. He'd kept their moneyman Charles Dunnwood as his accountant. At this point, with the long-term investments from the big Google and Qualcomm payouts, along with a slew of stocks that Dunnwood controlled, Ducky had nothing to worry about.

But rather than live a cushy life of excess, he created something of a burgeoning empire that, if found out by the authorities, would land him in prison for the rest of his life, where he would likely end up on the business end of a shank before anyone even had a chance to rape him raw. Convicts didn't take kindly to baby killers.

As Ducky walked the hall of champions upstairs, he cradled the new baby like a proud father, smiling into his cherub face and cooing. The walls of the hall were lined with pictures of babies after their victories, some sweaty and bruised, others caked with the blood of their fallen opponents. One baby had an eye completely swollen shut, her little ear swelled up like a deformed cauliflower, mouth hanging in a toothless snarl. Every time Ducky passed that portrait he looked upon the greatest champ he'd ever seen and it took his breath away. That was a fight he'd never forget. Like a junkie chasing that dragon, looking for an even better high, Ducky was always seeking out another champion.

He held up his newest acquisition and smiled at the boy.

Maybe this will be the one that takes Barbarella down.

Cradling the baby in his left arm, Ducky opened the door to nursery room one. Inside were four cribs lining the walls and a baby-changing table pushed up into a corner beside the closet door. At the moment, there was no nurse working for Ducky. The last one, Susan Fairmount, had to be exterminated. It had been very tense. Ducky thought she would be able to keep his secret, but she was becoming too attached to the children. Ryan had found her outside of a biker bar in El Cajon. She'd been a real tough cookie, a straight up biker bitch with attitude and real grit. The kind of woman who would work for something as depraved as baby fights and not flinch, but over the course of six months something in her changed. The biker persona was just that. A persona. Deep down she was a loving woman who had gone so far off the rails of excess and fun, she'd become callous. Spending so much time with babies brought out a maternal instinct no one thought existed within her.

She'd become particularly close to a baby Ryan and Chance abducted in Santee. A baby girl they called Storm. It was the first girl they'd had in a while, at least the first girl in nursery one. Something about Storm reminded Susan of her own daughter, taken away by CPS at age two when Susan was helplessly addicted to meth. She'd kicked meth after a near death experience, but never kicked the drinking or the lifestyle, thus never got her child back. Susan thought she didn't want her child back. That was, until Storm came into her life.

The night Storm was up for her first fight, Susan cried and cried. She'd never actually seen the fights, but understood what they were. She didn't see the aftermath either, only working in nursery one. The champs resided in nursery two, on the other side of the Jack and Jill bathroom, and the losers never made it back to either nursery.

That night, Storm didn't make it back.

Worse than that, Susan, eager to find out if the little girl she'd become so attached to had survived, stood at the window that looked down into the backyard where the arena had been built. She saw Ryan carrying a bloody baby, and though she had seen this before, and though it had affected her, she'd always been able to turn away and pretend the things she knew had been happening hadn't happened at all. This time, she knew who the baby was. She knew it was Storm, and she broke down.

By the time Ducky and Chance had come in, exhausted and buzzing with adrenaline from the fights, they discovered Susan scrambling at the front door with two crying babies in the crooks of her arms.

"What the fuck are you doing?" Ducky asked.

Susan stopped, her whole body quivering, and turned to face the demon baby murderers who she'd foolishly trusted. In that moment Susan felt a great shame that she'd somehow got involved in all of this. She also felt a pang or regret and a load of fear, for she knew that there was no way she was getting out of there. Too much was at stake. She'd seen too much, *knew* too much, and people who had no heart regarding the lives of babies would kill a woman without thinking.

"Grab the babies," Ducky said as he stared Susan in the eyes. It was a terrifying stare, one that Susan had never seen from Ducky. Intense. Determined. Mad with something only the very privileged possess when they've gotten everything they've ever wanted and finally saw something unraveling.

Susan gripped the babies tight, but loosened her grip, realizing their lives meant nothing to Chance and Ducky. They were no better than dogs. She could have put up more of a fight, but they'd have yanked the babies out of her grasp, and that could have been disastrous.

Chase took the children and went upstairs.

Ducky approached Susan, who, at that point, had begun to whimper and plead for her life. The typical "just let me go, I won't tell anyone" stuff. Ducky reached up and grabbed a tuft of hair from the back of her head. Her hands darted up, wrapping around the fist that gripped a ball of her hair tight. He gritted his teeth, eyes blazing as he stared into hers. The eyes of a maniac. A rotten, stinking, privileged madman. He slammed her face into the massive, solid wood front door. After the first hit she screamed. *Smash!* Then she cried out in horror. *Smash!* Then she whimpered.

Ducky slammed her face into that door repeatedly until she was quieted, which took a hell of a lot more slams than he had anticipated. Susan held on for dear life, as if she had something to live for. She held on for a future that would never materialize. For a family she would never have the opportunity to love. Once she went limp and he realized that he was holding up her dead weight, Ducky let go. Susan's body fell to the mosaic-tiled entryway with a thump that echoed, bouncing off the stained vaulted ceiling. Her face was bloody from the broken nose and bits of skull that splintered and ripped through her flesh. One of her eyes had ruptured, leaking ocular fluid that mixed with the blood rapidly pooling beneath her.

Ducky thought about that night often, especially when he went up to nursery one. He'd liked Susan, but she'd revealed a major flaw in his plans. Trust. How could he trust anyone? Even trusting Ryan and

Chance was iffy. They were insane. They'd done terrible things. Ducky had all kinds of evidence against them, and he made sure they were aware of that fact. But how would he get another nanny to watch over the babies?

Ducky had enjoyed the feeling of slamming Susan's face into the door. He'd liked the blood. It was a wonderful release, and even more exciting having come on the heels of a successful Baby Fight. But Ducky was no killer. Well, he was, but not a serial killer. He may have taken pleasure in what he'd done, but he wasn't about to become an American Psycho. At least not that variety.

Placing the new baby boy in a vacant cradle, Ducky wondered if this one would become the new champ. Baby Fight champs didn't last long. Their little developing bodies could only handle so much before they just broke down. Those were some of the worst fights. Ducky had to be more wary of what the champions could handle. On the other hand, when a champ went down, things got ugly, and that was a major draw to these kinds of illegal and illicit activities. Some of his clientele loved seeing a champ wiped out in grand fashion. The bloodier, the better.

The baby started crying. Ducky looked into the crib with something like amusement, deep in thought.

The other babies in the room had been sleeping too. They were awakened, one by one, from the wailing of the new arrival. Soon, the entire room was filled with crying babies. Four in all. Ducky grabbed a small diffuser like what perfume came in. He gave one spray over the crib of each baby, watching the mist as it floated down onto their little faces.

As Ducky left the room, he said, "Sweet nightmares."

He dusted them with a heavily diluted dose of LSD.

Five

Madison saw her father and felt a great deal of shame. It was in his eyes, the look he gave her that caused this feeling to rear its ugly head once again. He'd been ashamed that his daughter had become pregnant out of wedlock. Ashamed that she picked a man who was such a gem that he disappeared at the mere mention of pregnancy.

Those shameful eyes. Forever burning. Staring holes into her soul.

"Should have made better decisions, Madison."

His hollow voice ringing in her mind like the tolling of some massive bell to remind her of her failures, as if no one was supposed to make mistakes, especially his little princess.

"We're not taking care of that kid, Madison." Cold eyes staring at her, judging her.

She'd never asked for that. His words haunted her. It was as if her father had assumed his "little princess" would come to them one day with pregnancy news before she had a ring on her finger, as if that was the be all and end all of her fucking life.

"You picked a real winner, Madison."

His eyes bored into her like flaming jewels.

Madison woke, and yet felt like she was still asleep. Her eyes refused to open properly and her brain felt as if it had been submerged in gummy taffy. At first it felt as if she'd been in one of those ultra-heavy sleeps she would get when she was a little girl, the type that resulted in a crust over her eyes so thick she could barely open them, but she hadn't slept like that in years, and she was no little girl. It only took a moment for her mind to catch up, and then Madison remembered what was going on.

She managed to open her eyes, but everything was blurry. Though she realized that she had been abducted and was in trouble, she was having a hard time piecing all the details together.

Panic rose within, but there was no way to release the surge. The bad vibes roiled up and were absorbed into her frantic mind, almost like hallucinations. Madison's thoughts tumbled in on one another. She saw her father's eyes like bizarre guideposts that led to nothing. She saw flashes of color. Flashes of conversation, voices she couldn't place.

And then she saw the Wal-Mart parking lot.

She saw Hunter taken from her.

Tears seeped out of Madison's eyes, rolling down her face and onto her body. She realized then that she was topless. She opened her eyes, but her vision remained gluey and blurred.

The room smelled stale, as if no one had been there for some time. Kind of like a shirt that sat at the bottom of the drawer for a year and gets that strange odor that isn't particularly bad, but not good either. It kind of reminded her of the spare bedroom in her grandparent's house that she would sleep in when her parents had gone on a trip by themselves. She'd always been kind of scared of Grandma's house for some reason. And the room she had to sleep in was stuck in a time warp, untouched since the sixties with shag carpet, mid-century furniture, framed pictures of Jesus and Elvis (as if they were one and the same, which her grandmother pretty much believed they were), and that damn musty old smell, only altered on occasion by the distinctive odor of mothballs.

So many strange visions and memories haunted Madison as she lay there. Finally her eyes somewhat adjusted to the dark. She worked on moving her limbs, but she was so drugged up that even basic motor skills were difficult.

Madison hadn't experimented much with drugs. She'd partied in college, but mostly drinking. She'd seen how crazy people got on pills and wanted no part of that. Alcohol was enough for her, and after a few years of partying, she'd had enough of *that* too. These days she would maybe have a glass of wine or the occasional beer, but that was the extent of her drinking.

As Madison began to trace the outlines of what little furniture was in the room, searching for a window (if there was one it had been covered with blackout blinds considering how dark the room was), the door opened, light spilling in as two men entered, one of them holding a baby.

Even through her drug haze, Madison could tell that it wasn't Hunter.

One of the guys, Chance, the one with the beard that she vaguely remembered from the Wal-Mart parking lot, turned on the light. The illumination caused Madison to clench her eyes tight as the flash of brightness seemed to shoot directly into her brain like red-hot pokers.

The other man moved forward, baby in his hands. He had a grin on him like he was enjoying every minute of his life as a babynapper.

"Baby gotta feed," Ryan said as he moved in closer to Madison.

"She's moving," Chance said. He watched from the doorway, worry in his eyes. "We need to give her another shot?"

Ryan tilted his head, staring at Madison on the futon where they deposited her a few hours ago. Ryan shook his head. "I don't think so. We don't want to give her an overdose. But be ready in case she comes to and starts anything." Ryan chuckled. "I like 'em feisty anyway."

As Ryan laid the baby on the futon beside Madison, placing the mouth to one of her breasts, Chance asked, "How long you think babies can feed after the mother dies?"

Ryan went rigid. Tilted his head to look over his shoulder. "What kind of dumbass question is that?" Then he squinted his eyes, thinking about the question. "I mean, I guess until she's out of milk. I suppose. It isn't like she'd be producing or anything, not if she's fucking dead."

The baby latched.

Ryan smiled. "See. I knew this was a good idea. This one's been crying and whining for days, not eating much of the formula we've been giving her. I swear to god, Chance, I almost throttled her little head off the other night. When is Ducky going to get another nanny? I'm getting tired of this shit."

Chance stood, scratched his head. "I don't know. After the last one, I guess he has to find the right fit."

"He'd better do it soon. I've had it up to here with this shit. I don't mind going out and getting babies, but this taking care of them shit is for the birds."

The conversation trickled into Madison's ears. She couldn't really feel the baby feeding, but felt pressure. Kind of like being under Novocain at the dentist's office. They didn't sound like goons from some TV show or movie. Their voices were like that of your average college student. Somewhat young and eager, well spoken, for the most part. They sounded kind of like yuppies or jocks.

Not entirely sure what was going on or what they had in store for her, Madison remained quiet. She tried to open her eyes a few times, but the drugs were still owning her body, restricting her movements, which might have been a good thing. They spoke of drugging her up more if needed. And Madison certainly did not need that.

Laying there with the strange numb sensation of a baby girl (*whose baby is feeding on my breast?*) latched onto her nipple, Madison feared the men whose voices drifted into her ears would then rape her. Or maybe they were disgusted by the feeder of babies, turned off by her mommy body. She hoped so. But moreover, she was fearful for what was happening to Hunter. What had they done with him? The urge to scream at these men, to ask where her baby was, intensified, but all she could do was moan and shift her body.

"I think she's coming to," Chance said, brandishing the syringe.

"Take it easy, bro. You can't just keep dosing her with that shit. Too much will kill her."

Chance grimaced, a sneer seen through the bush of his beard. "Too much my ass."

Madison decided to lie there until the men left. If another dose didn't kill her, it would certainly turn her into even more of a vegetable than she felt already.

Six

After putting the baby girl (she'd been renamed Athena, after the Greek goddess of war) back into the nursery and giving her a spritz with the LSD infused mist, Ryan went outside, slipping into the pool house unseen by the others. They were in the arena, a large indoor pool, only the water had been drained from the pool, and it had been fitted with lighting. That's where the fights were held.

The old pool house had been a changing room back when Ducky's parents were alive that had since been ignored. Ryan had Ducky order a deep freezer for the waste after a successful fight. Ryan's plan was to freeze the dead babies, the losers, and when there were enough to make it worth the hassle, he would place them into an ice chest and visit a friend Ryan had who worked at a funeral home. This friend owed Ryan big time. All Ryan asked was for the use of the incinerator from time to time, no questions asked. It was a total *Return of the Living Dead* deal, and the guy was cool enough to nod his head and ask no questions. When Ryan dropped by, he always joked that he had another load of rabid weasels.

But Ryan hadn't been to see that particular friend in quite some time.

Ryan opened the door. The smell of the pool house hit him full in the face. It was a smell most found repugnant, but he relished in, and he wasn't entirely sure why. He quickly closed the door, fearful that the odor would escape and lure someone to his retreat. Ducky was oblivious, rarely even walking around the backside of the arena, but Ryan had smelt the pool house from across the backyard. Just a whiff. The pool house was backed up to wooded public land. When anyone mentioned the smell, Ryan was prompt to blame the dried up creek bed. He claimed that's where coyotes fed, leaving the scraps of their meals to rot.

Once inside the pool house, Ryan gazed upon his art. He'd gone to college to study art. His parents paid his way, paying enough to get a no-talent hack into one of the best art schools in the country. Ryan did the whole alpha cappa delta college fraternity bullshit, but not only was he a shit artist, he didn't really get along with his fraternity brothers either, especially the hazing. Ryan knew that hazing was a rite of passage, but he loathed being bullied and made to feel low. One night the freshmen were all put into a room and blindfolded. Ryan didn't like the way things had been shaping up. Then the freshmen were made to have a sort of eating contest. Tasting food and guessing what it was. A correct guess and the blindfold came off. Of course, the food wasn't food at all. One fraternity brother shoved his finger up his own ass and stuck it onto a freshman's mouth. Another Found an old cigarette butt that had been outside for who knew how long.

One freshman was made to drink a cup of phlegmy spit. Another got a spoonful of cat food.

Ryan ended up with Derek Porter's dick in his mouth. He thought it was a sausage, but then the laughing gave it away. Derek was one of the top dogs in the fraternity. A real asshole prick who got his jollies off of making the freshmen suffer, as if he were making up for a life of abuse handed down from his old man. Derek said something like "give it to me, daddy" and Ryan knew he was sucking dick. His pride got the better of him. He bit down on that cock like a junkyard dog. Derek jumped back, but the damage had been done. There were teeth marks and blood.

They gave Ryan a beating. Derek had to get stitches in his rod. The beating wasn't so bad. Better than dick stitches.

Soon after, Ryan dropped out. His artistic abilities were pathetic at the very best. The other students in his classes were talking shit behind his back. Once word got around that his parents had bribed the school to enroll him, they were vicious.

Ryan had fantasized about making art with the blood from his enemies. In his mind's eye he was Picasso, painting abstract pictures in red, using bits of flesh and ropes of intestine to give the artwork a three dimensional pop. Or maybe he could do one of those simple yet effective pieces like Andreas Serrano was known for. Derek's crudely extracted penis tacked to an old piece of plywood, tufts of curly hair jutting out all dried with his blood. Maybe paint 12 through 11 around it and call the piece "Wall Cock".

When Ryan arrived back to San Diego he was a different man. His artistic taste had gone sour and completely bent. He knew he was a disappointment to his parents, and he didn't care. It was too difficult for them to continue arguing with him about his future, so they eventually conceded and allowed him to live in the guesthouse, although he spent most of his time at Ducky's place.

When Ryan felt down, he came to the pool house and stared at his artwork. Genius wasn't always immediately appreciated, and sometimes not in the creator's lifetime. Many a genius artist died poor. Ryan wouldn't die poor, considering he came from money, but there was a distinct possibility he would die before his genius could be recognized.

Closing his eyes, Ryan shuddered. Sometimes he would get a feeling like *deja vu* that would come over him like an avalanche of emotion, and in that moment he would see things as they really were. In that moment, that fraction of a second, he would pity himself, as if his conscience was trapped somewhere within his mind, rapping on the folds of his brain for attention. A mere glimpse of sane reasoning, a bastard recollection of right and wrong.

Ryan left the pool house to compose himself. There was a fight later, and he had to be prepared.

If everything went the way he hoped, tonight he would create.

Seven

By the third baby, Madison wanted to scream.

Feeding Hunter would sometimes cause her breasts to become sore, especially when he was hungry and eager. The babies these men were bringing in seemed as if they hadn't eaten in days. Three in a row and it felt as if Madison's nipples were going to fall off. One of them gnawed on her nipple like it was teething. Her body tensed and quivered from the pain, but she managed to remain as if in a drug haze despite tears that squeezed out of her listless eyes.

Between visits, she worked at moving her arms enough to massage her aching breasts. It was a minor respite, but welcomed for more reasons than mere relief. As the drugs they'd injected her with wore off, she began to feel aches in her body from the contorted position she'd been lying in. Madison twisted herself into as much a comfortable position as she could, but as soon as there was movement at the door, she'd go limp.

The last two visits had only been one man, the one with the beard and the weird cigarette always dangling from his maw, never lit. He must have been one of those people who quit smoking but insisted on carrying one around for comfort. Madison watched him through the slits of her eyelids, mimicking the look of someone deep in the throes of a drug haze. He scrutinized her deeply, as if trying to judge whether he should give her another shot of morphine or oxy or whatever. Madison was no actor, but she hoped her performance worked. She figured some people have a very low tolerance for drugs. Just so long as she could continue to convince them she was one of those people, she had a chance at escaping.

The third baby was much gentler than the previous two, but the shape it was in almost caused Madison to cry out. Its head was misshapen with welts and bumps and scattered with bruises that varied from deep purple to faded green. One of the baby's eyes was swollen closed and oozing pus, but the other gazed up at her as it fed, all red with busted capillaries. Its body was a map of healing wounds, cuts, and abrasions. A particularly nasty gash in the side of its cheek was puffy and red in desperate need of stitches.

As it fed, Madison watched Chance puff on that unlit cigarette, anything to take her mind off of the state of the baby. She noticed that the filter had red lipstick on it. She almost cringed at the sight, but kept her dopey composure. Something about the red lipstick grossed her out, as if he'd found the cigarette on the ground, tossed there from some random woman.

The more Madison thought about it, the more she wondered what the deal with the cigarette was.

Chance stared down at her. She could tell that his eyes were seeing through her, as if imagining something else. Madison didn't like that look. She'd never been sexually assaulted, but somehow she thought that was the look of someone considering very bad things. He tilted his head just a bit, that nasty cigarette dangling out of his mouth, just enough for the red lipstick to be seen.

Madison hoped and prayed the baby would finish and start whining so Chance would have to take it out of the room and she would have some peace. He'd been in there three times, and each time he became creepier, especially that blank stare. There was something seriously wrong with this guy.

He withdrew the cigarette and examined it as if having some sort of strange epiphany. He then reached out, cigarette in hand, and placed the thing to Madison's lips, wedging it between them until it stayed in place.

Inside she screamed, but couldn't let it show, not even in her eyes. If he saw even the slightest movement from her he would drug her again.

Chance looked on, mouth hanging open through the groomed tangles of his beard.

The cigarette was wet at the end, which gave Madison a squirming sensation that she used all her might to fight off. But something was strange about it. It felt wrong. She had never been a smoker, but had indulged a few times in high school with friends. The filter didn't feel right. It was as if the cigarette was encased in something. Wax or resin or something. It looked so real, but she was convinced Chance carted around a fake cigarette. One with red lipstick on it.

What a fucking freak.

BABY FIGHTS

When the baby became fussy, Chance snatched the cigarette out of Madison's mouth and then did the same with the baby. She couldn't take another moment of either the battered infant or that damn cigarette. After he was gone, she sat in the dark room and cried.

Chance was fucking with her. Next time she would have to make a move, or else he was going to be the one to make a move, and she didn't want that no matter *what* his next move was.

Eight

Chance closed the door, gripping Jenny's cigarette tight between his lips. He closed his eyes and shuddered as a couple of tears squeezed their way through his clenched eyelids and slid down his cheeks and into his beard. He held the baby to his chest like a father, somehow finding comfort it the warmth of its little body. Ducky had named this one Zoltar. Chance didn't get the reference.

It wasn't that the woman in the room reminded him of Jenny, at least not her hair color or even her body shape. There was something about the woman. Maybe the hint of red lipstick on her lips. Maybe it was her nose, or even her facial structure. There was something.

Chance had never allowed anyone to touch Jenny's cigarette, much less put it onto their mouth like that. He wasn't even sure what compelled him to do so. It felt like a betrayal to the only woman he'd ever loved.

Holding the baby in one arm, Chance pulled the cigarette out of his mouth between middle and pointer finger, as if he were smoking it. He examined the cancer stick, the pattern of Jenny's red lips left on the filter. Her final kiss. Chance had the cigarette encased in resin to protect it. He wished he could suck air through it, as if getting to inhale Jenny's essence, but this was the best way to preserve her memory.

Chance had found the cigarette still clinging to Jenny's lips when he found her body. He took it before the police and paramedics arrived. He knew she was gone. He and Jenny had been high school sweethearts. They'd learned about life together, about love, about everything. He knew she had bouts of depression. He knew they could get bad. But he hadn't been prepared for that day. Jenny had been so happy just the day before. Happier than Chance could remember, and that had made him feel good. He'd felt positive about their future together, that maybe they were turning a corner in their relationship. Having been together since high school, Jenny had wondered if they'd missed something by not dating other people. She would mention this to Chance, and though he felt opposite, his love for Jenny like an undying flame, he could see that she felt trapped. That day before she killed herself she didn't seem trapped at all. That day was amazing. It was like having the Jenny he'd met in school back.

"Hey, what the fuck are you doing, man?"

Chance turned to see Ryan coming up the stairs. Chance shook his head. "Nothing. Just thinking."

"You better get your head out of the clouds, bro. I see you get caught in your thoughts like that way too much. Let her go, dude. You can start by throwing away that fucking cigarette."

"Shut your fucking mouth."

Ryan snickered. "Don't act tough with me. Do yourself a favor and smoke that thing. It'll do you good. Maybe you can finally forget and move on with your life."

Chance tightened his lips, concealing them with his beard, and his eyes went to mere slits, as if trying desperately to show his anger. He turned and walked baby Zoltar to nursery number two, where he disappeared through the door, leaving Ryan with that big shit-eating grin he always had on his face.

Chance was beginning to hate Ryan, and he was *especially* beginning to hate that fucking grin. Ryan thought a lot of himself. Mr. Perfect. Well fuck that. *Let's see him find his girlfriend dead and laugh about it!*

"Hey!"

Chance stopped in his tracks, just inside the doorway to nursery two. He hated that tone in Ryan's voice. It was condescending. Ryan acted as if he were a superior to Chance, when they both knew they were in the same boat here. Ducky ran the show. He played no favorites, at least not that Chance could see.

Chance peeked out of the room and down the hall, baby still cradled in his arms.

Ryan's grin had evened out some, showing irritation. "Bring out Xena. She's up tonight against Sherman." Now the grin was back. "Fuckin' Sherman. Where the hell does Ducky come up with this shit."

Nine

From outside, the arena looked like nothing special. Just an outbuilding, an enclosed pool, which was something more commonly found in eastern states than in California. The windows had been blacked out to eliminate any light from escaping, giving the building the constant look of being out of use, even in the middle of the night. A nosey neighbor, one who used binoculars considering how far the arena was from the nearest neighbor, wouldn't be able to tell that Baby Fights took place within these walls.

Inside, Ducky chummed it up with the men and women who paid top dollar to observe and bet on the fights. The price for admission was five grand a head. The wagers were even steeper, this assuring that at least one of them walked away with a profit. The others enjoyed both the brutal sensationalism of the act, as well as the gamble. Baby Fights were not for just any person, but the person who had everything and wanted something more, something they couldn't get elsewhere. Baby Fights was something people only spoke of in hushed tones, and only with those who they knew were into such abstract and depraved forms of entertainment.

These days, Ducky didn't even actively seek out customers. They came to him, and when they did they had better have a sponsor, else he denied everything and threatened legal action for harassment and defamation. On top of that, he would find out who sent someone to him without a sponsor and threaten them with blackmail.

Ducky had something on every single patron of his precious Baby Fights. He'd designed the interview process that way, much like the interview he'd done with the newest member, Theresa Gibson.

Ducky was always a bit shocked when a woman joined the ranks of his patrons. He couldn't imagine any woman so depraved and sick that she would enjoy a blood sport such as Baby Fights. Those types of women intrigued and frightened Ducky. But he was an equal opportunity type of guy and would allow anyone to partake, so far as they have the money and pass the interview. Theresa checked both of those boxes. The interview, despite a number of questions that were vague and in no way incriminating to Ducky, always ended with him taking a video. That's where things could get dicey. People, even those who were into some of the sickest shit imaginable, did not like having things out in the world, things out of their control, that were as incriminating as what Ducky demanded of them.

It was like some new small-timer buying large amounts of drugs from one of the big-time dealers. They couldn't just go into that sort of deal without proving they weren't cops, and proving was sampling the goods. It was rare an undercover officer would take a hit of top shelf crystal just to stay in character, especially since most undercover officers didn't do drugs. It was a sure way for a drug dealer to weed out their clientele.

With Theresa, Ducky had pulled out his phone, set it on a tripod, and started filming her. He then handed Theresa a baby. One of the warrior babies, bruised and swollen from battle in the arena. The look on her face was something like amused disgust. Prior to Ducky starting the video, they'd talked about what he expected from her. Just one act of violence perpetrated on the baby and she was in. The baby was damaged as it were, and Theresa being in the video with a baby in such a state was enough for blackmail, but she had to do something to the infant, that way it didn't look like a setup.

Most of the videos that Ducky had saved in a series of encrypted files on several devices showed his patrons slapping, punching, or even choking babies. Theresa went one step further. In a move Ducky could never have prepared himself for, Theresa palmed the back of the baby's head with one hand. A look of madness came over her, eyes wide and glaring, teeth bared. She then latched her teeth onto the baby's face, kind of snarled, and pulled away, revealing a chunk of nose that had been removed. The baby screamed and flailed and Theresa almost dropped it onto the ground. Blood dotted her mouth. She started chewing on the nose, and then spit it out. She looked at Ducky, who promptly turned off the video feed.

Even now, as Ducky yucked it up with his guests, he was wary of Theresa. She was a wild card, and every bit welcome to bet on Baby Fights. He assumed she would become a regular.

Also in attendance was Joseph Kisner, an older gentleman who owned a baseball team, a yacht, and was known to poach game in Africa, where he boasted about narrowly escaping death at the hands of a group of Africans who poached the poachers, a story he told with relish to anyone who would listen. David Yasmin was a Baby Fights regular, a younger entrepreneur who made his fortune off a number of cheap products that had ruled infomercials and social media ads for years. He'd since invested his earnings elsewhere and was rumored to have hundreds of millions tucked away in offshore accounts. Sandra Vermillion was the only other woman in attendance besides Theresa, she having swindled several rich men out of their very livelihoods and money. People joked behind her back, calling her the Black Widow. She was coy, but had been the second most brutal during her blackmail video.

Altogether there were seven patrons on this fine night, eager for some excitement. There were wagers on more than just the outcome. With only seven patrons the odds were very different from betting on the ponies, for instance. They placed bets on which baby would be first to attack, which would bleed first, which would cry first, which would piss or shit first (two separate bets). The outcome of each fight was worth the most money, but all of the little bets added up, creating a more enjoyable experience, although, for these people, the experience of watching babies fight to the death was like no other. That was the true draw.

Like horse races, everyone was given little pamphlets with specs on each of the babies who would be fighting tonight. Name, weight, ethnicity, history in the ring, that sort of thing. The bets were listed, and wagers made. On arrival, the patrons would read the information in silence as they made their wagers. There was a great deal of scrutiny. Early arrivals spent more time with the pamphlet, really trying to get an understanding of which babies they would choose for winners.

As they sipped cocktails and puffed designer vape pens, they chatted about the type of things people discussed while at a cocktail party, as if they weren't all there to witness a gruesome underground bloodsport. There was a bent feeling of morbid excitement in the air, but no one addressed it. No one spoke of their bets. No one even spoke of previous fights, as if because what they were involved in was deeply illegal, it was better to experience the fights than discuss them openly.

Ryan popped into the arena to a small gathering of smiling people, most of whom he'd seen before.

"We'll begin in ten minutes," Ryan said.

The patrons murmured in response, all smiles and anticipation.

Ten

Ducky stood on the balcony outside his master quarters, overlooking the backyard. He gazed upon his little arena of violence, wondering what it was his patrons talked about while waiting for something as sick and depraved as watching babies fight to the death. He often wondered what kind of people were into this sort of thing, something that was revealed to him when interviewing potential patrons, and taking the blackmail video. People were willing to tie themselves to this stuff just to participate. They themselves were sick and demented. They had everything in the world, and everything was not enough. Ducky understood. He was one of them.

He'd started small with dogfights. What Ducky didn't like was dealing with animals. There was this whole underground culture revolving around dogfights that Ducky had no interest in. People not only bred pit bulls for fighting, they trained them for it. Ducky wasn't even close to interested enough to train animals, and he found that there were far less people interested in watching untrained dogs go after one another. He started setting up unique dogfights, avoiding pit bulls by opting for Chihuahuas and other smaller breeds that were known for being aggressive. He'd taunt them and keep them hungry, hoping they would be angry and starved and put up a good fight.

Dogfight purists were into pits. They were into it as a bloodsport. They wanted to watch the most vicious animals tear one another apart, and they got off on it. Smaller breeds weren't cutting it, and it wasn't what Ducky wanted. He was drawn to the fights because he enjoyed seeing two beings rage against one another, but something was missing.

One day Ducky was waiting for a flight at the airport and saw a mother trying desperately to console her baby who was putting up a hell of a fight. The kid slapped at its mother and kicked and had a look on its little face like anger incarnate. Ducky's life changed in that moment. He realized his calling. He'd never given a damn about babies. Never wanted to have children. He wasn't even sure he wanted marriage. He wasn't so much a womanizer as he liked women who were interested in sex as a sport rather than pursuing love. He lived for pleasure, and being a man who'd always had everything handed to him, he had to go to some pretty bizarre places to hit those pleasure centers in his mind. Regular relationships didn't do it for him. Even his sex life was becoming more and more violent. He would seek out women who wanted to be hit. Women who wanted to be used. Women with low self-esteem. For a while he had this little junkie girl who would do anything he asked just so long as he gave her a fix in return. The longer she went without a fix, the more eager she was to engage in risky, bizarre sexual behaviors. Eventually Ducky grew bored of seeing her face and had Ryan and Chance drop her off somewhere downtown.

There was a light rap on the door. From the other side came Ryan's voice. "On in five minutes."

"I'll be down," Ducky said.

Ducky stared out of the window some more, watching as Ryan entered the covered pool that served as the arena. He sipped iced water. He had no regrets.

Eleven

The vibe during Baby Fights was unlike a boxing match or wrestling match in that there were only so many people in attendance, and though they were excited for the spectacle, and some of them were intoxicated or otherwise stimulated, there weren't enough of them to create a roaring crowd. One thing about a live event was the roaring crowd. It was infectious. A good crowd made a fan out of a casual observer. At Baby Fights there were no casual observers. There were only people heavily vested in the night's events, and so even when it was quiet, that was not an indication that things were going awry or people weren't enjoying themselves. It was anticipation, something of a rarity during most live sports.

Ducky entered the arena to claps and cheers. He wasn't one to crave attention, but he also did not shy away from it. He was just as much an eager observer as his guests. It wasn't the money or the power that he strived for. It was the thrill.

"I'm so glad you all could join us this evening," Ducky said. "Good to see you, Joseph. It's been a while. Don't be a stranger."

Joseph smiled and nodded.

"Sandra," Ducky said, smiling, "you look lovely tonight. Try not to get any blood spatter on that dress."

Sandra laughed. "All that would do is make a new fashion statement."

"Right you are. You've all made bets, I can see. The first match of the night pits Xena versus Sherman. Sherman is new to the fights. I named duly, as I'm sure you can guess considering how big he is. Built like a Sherman tank."

Chuckles all around.

"But," Ducky raised his eyebrows and paused, recapturing everyone's attention. "Does he have what it takes to make his way to the top? Barbarella is the reigning champion, and she will fight tonight. But ask yourself, does Sherman have what it takes to take her crown?"

The babies crawled around the shallow end of the drained pool of which the patrons sat around. Inside the pool with them was Chance, acting as a herder of sorts to keep the babies to one side as they waited for the fights to begin.

"Theresa is the newest member of this most exclusive club," Ducky said. "Everyone, give her a round of applause, if you will."

The others golf-clapped for Theresa. She smiled curtly, almost bashful of the spotlight being directed towards her.

"You would cringe if you knew what she did on her introduction video." Ducky smiled, his lips twisted into his namesake duck-like sneer. "You'll enjoy this, Theresa. I know it." Ducky pulled a syringe from the pocket of his coat. "You all know how this works, but I like to keep new patrons informed. This is a little rundown for Theresa."

Ducky directed his attention straight at Theresa, who again seemed uncomfortable, as if the spotlight were again on her, which was normal for a first-timer. It was a rare occasion people engaged in such activities in groups of strangers. There was a sense of danger that was both frightening and exhilarating.

"In this syringe," Ducky said, "is a microdose of angel dust."

Theresa's eyes deepened. Ducky smiled.

"I see the gut reaction plastered across your face, Theresa. I also know that you are very aware of what is going to happen tonight, so it should come to you as no surprise that we have to do something to stimulate aggression within the infants who have been chosen to fight. Aggression isn't something naturally present in babies. Put two of them together in an empty pool such as this and they will coo and gurgle and play together, but that's no fun.

"When I was thinking of a way to make an infant as riled up and mean as a starved pit bull, I remembered a video I had once seen about a man who was high on angel dust. He was out of his mind, walking around naked and bloody from whatever insanity he'd gotten into while higher than the clouds in the sky. At one point he climbed up a telephone pole naked. One of those old log telephone poles, all dried out and splintering like mad. Nails and staples and shit in it at the bottom from garage sale and missing dog signs. Guy climbs up the thing and that looks like it hurts. He's like a fucking ape, the way he climbs. Finally the police show up. They convince him down, and do you know what the crazy, drugged out son of a bitch does?"

Theresa shook her head. The others smile grimly, having heard the story at least once before.

"The fucker *slides* down the telephone pole like he's going down a fireman's pole. By the time he gets to the bottom his groin and stomach is nothing but a mass of blood and splinters of all sizes. I'm convinced he left his junk somewhere on the pole in shreds of his manhood. Crazy, yet, the guy was still out of control. It took ten police officers to hold him down. Why they didn't use lethal force, I'll never know."

Ducky took a deep breath.

"Anyway, that's where I got the idea that a micro dose of angel dust—the good shit, pure freebase—would turn even a baby into a killing machine."

"Why babies?" Theresa asked. Her lips curled in something close to a sneaky smile, the grin of a woman whose late night proclivities were dark and held close to the heart.

Ducky sort of chuckled. "Get two men high on angel dust in a ring and it would be a hell of a fight, but I don't know anyone who wants to deal with the winner. A baby, we can deal with."

Theresa nodded.

"Also," Ducky added, "I feel this is more entertaining. More . . . unexpected."

Lips pursed, eyes raised, Theresa said, "I certainly hope so."

"You won't be disappointed."

"We've tattooed an X on Xena's forehead, so there isn't any confusion, though you can see that she's darker skinned than Sherman. And, of course, their diapers have been removed, so there is an anatomical difference that distinguishes the two."

BABY FIGHTS

"Tattooed a baby?" David said, a look on his face like someone suggested they do body shots from his mother's wrinkled belly button.

"For fuck's sake, David, you've been here before. It gets so much worse than a tattoo."

Soft chuckles from the crowd. They all looked into the empty pool, into the pit. Xena looked up, her face chubby and red in places where cuts from her previous fight had healed. The tattooed X was sloppy, as if done with a homemade tattoo gun by a total amateur. Despite the baby girl having battled before, she looked like an average, curious infant. One eye was droopy, from a nasty blow, but she'd pulled through.

Sherman was unscathed, completely oblivious to what was about to happen. He could have been used in a Gerber's baby food ad.

"Let the first fight begin," Ducky said, handing the syringe to Ryan. "Give them the jab."

Ryan nodded and took the steps into the shallow end of the empty pool, syringe in hand. He worked quickly as he grabbed first Sherman's and then Xena's arms, driving the needle into their flesh and depressing the plunger. The babies cried, and then cries turned to full-blown whaling.

One of the guests cringed, but it was impossible to tell whether the response was in sympathy or an adversity to the sound of a howling infant. Probably the latter, all things considered.

"Give it a moment," Ducky said, more to Theresa than the others who had been to previous matches.

Ducky smiled. This part never ceased to excite him. The look in the babies' eyes when the freebase took hold, it was magic. Licking his lips in anticipation, everything seemed to stop, as it did every week during the fights. The feeling wasn't akin to sexual release, but more like the endorphin rush from some kind of drug. Like Huey Louis and the News sang about, only it wasn't love for a woman, but the love for engaging in something heinous, something so lowdown and dirty even the most depraved sex acts couldn't scratch that particular itch.

Then it happened. The tightly scrunched up eyes of the babies popped open as some kind of recognition took hold in their little brains. The tears stopped. The crying stopped. Their eyes widened, the pupils reduced to pin points.

The patrons watched in awe.

Xena began twitching as if she'd grabbed a live wire, her tiny muscles beginning to spasm wildly. Sherman flopped onto his back, hitting his head on the concrete bottom of the drained pool, but not even cringing. He, too, trembled and shook as if having a seizure, which might have been exactly what was going on. Then Sherman twisted around, placing himself on hands and knees. The weight of his head seemed like a feat in itself, the thing bobbing and swaying as he maneuvered for purchase on limbs that threatened to fail him.

Xena, noticing her counterpart on the move, grimaced, mouth slightly open to reveal soft pink gums and an excess of saliva that ran out of her maw like a hungry dog faced with a bucket of fried chicken. Eyes impossibly wide, she locked onto her opponent and moved forward.

Sherman continued struggling to remain on all fours, head bobbing, which must have looked like a punching bag to Xena. She crawled up and gave him a good smack, right on the side of his head. Sherman made an odd squeal and went down, collapsing under the weight of his body and the disorientation of the drug.

Xena, face tightened into a bizarre display of preternatural hatred, something deep in the genetic makeup for her behaviors could not, at such a young age, have been learned, leapt onto Sherman with an animal growl.

The patrons gasped and even chuckled.

Not understanding or knowing how to ball her fists, Xena slapped at Sherman repeatedly. Finally the freebase came alive in Sherman's veins and he pushed Xena hard, launching her backwards and off balance. She fell, hitting her head on the concrete. Mustard-colored shit squeezed out with a wet fart. Sherman stood on two legs, but could only manage a stance for mere seconds before collapsing, catching his fall on arms that were red from getting slapped by Xena.

Sherman crawled to Xena, who was recovering from her fall, and grabbed at her face, taking a handful of her nose. She screeched in response, tried to pull away, but Sherman had a death grip on her schnoz. Xena shook her head back and forth, finally pulling out of Sherman's grip. Blood began gushing down her face from her crooked little nose.

Up on her feet, Xena took several steps forward and launched herself at Sherman. They punched and kicked and gummed one another like a couple of dogs during a fateful meeting. Savage blows, skin slapping skin, hands grasping and pulling, legs kicking. Angry sounds interspersed with random squeals or cries. Their skin became reddened from equal parts drug and physical abuse. The squeals turned to primal roars no one in the audience had heard from a babe's mouth. Blood leaked from ears and eyes and noses, smearing the two of them like strawberry jam. The concrete became slathered in baby blood.

Finally, Xena managed to get on top of Sherman. She still wasn't balling her fists, but that didn't matter. She had one hand on his jaw, holding him as still as she could even though he had her fingers clasped between his bloody gums. Her other hand swung at his face repeatedly, smacking him hard with her palm like a bludgeon tool as she made a hissing sound.

Sherman wrapped his mouth on her fingers as his head was ground into the rough concrete bottom of the empty pool, tearing skin and downy hair. He clenched his eyes tight and bit down. Xena screamed as she pulled her hand away, ripping two tiny fingers off, clenched tight between Sherman's gums, blood spurting from the raw stubs of flesh she whipped around wildly.

The patrons watching from what they thought was a safe distance got a scare as blood flew through the air, dotting the side of the pool.

Xena redirect her battering hands to focus on the source of her pain: Sherman's mouth. She smacked and beat on his mouth with both her good hand and the one missing a few digits, both of which slipped out of his bloody maw in a thick slime of pink mucus and saliva. When Sherman's jaw broke, he went into a tizzy, his legs beating the concrete wildly like a baby in a tantrum over the loss of a binky, the heels of his feet torn and bloody from their concrete battleground.

Swatting his balled fist at Xena in a last ditch effort to get her off of him, she took a few hard blows to the face, which knocked her off balance, toppling Xena. Sherman rolled over and got into a crawling position. He lifted his head and looked up at the observers, all of whom were stunned into silence. Sherman's face was a contortion, his jaw mangled and twisted, but still connected by the skin of his chin, though broken bones had punctured the flesh, a white shard jutting out of the gore. He was the visage of some overgrown abortion resurrected from a biohazard.

Despite her missing fingers and the welts that were forming on her head and arms, Xena was far less affected. She came after Sherman for a final attack. The strength in her little chubby arms was wild. This time she grabbed Sherman's mangled jaw and pulled. The rip where bone had breached flesh tore even more, but his jaw remained attached to his face. Sherman put up a fight, swinging his fists, but there was too much blood in his eyes and he was no match for a champion. Xena grabbed the piece of jawbone that protruded from his face and yanked, tearing the ripped flesh of his cheek wide open and removing the thing with a strength no baby should possess. Holding the extracted jaw, all pink with his bloody gums, she used the jagged end and began slashing at Sherman's gut, as if recognizing that the soft of his stomach was a weak point. Sherman lay there still and dead as baby Xena ripped open his gut with the jagged end of his own jawbone. Once the piñata was opened, she dropped the jaw and played with the warm, steaming prizes within. Removing chunky entrails with gleeful vigor, she wrapped his intestines around her body like a boa made of viscera.

Ducky stood tall and proud, a grin on his face like a junkie who'd just scored the purest of drugs. Gasps from his patrons gave him joy like no other. They came for a show, and that's exactly what they got.

"How's that for the first match?" Ducky said.

Theresa looked at him and nodded her approval, she the only one in attendance who remained stoic. One attendee had removed himself from the arena to vomit outside. Others wore looks on their faces like they had seen, well, exactly what they had seen.

"This far exceeds my wildest expectations," Theresa said.

Ducky nodded. "Good. The night is young." He then announced to the entire crowd, "The next match begins in half an hour."

As Chance sedated Xena and wrapped her in a blanket, Ryan was busy removing the dead baby by putting the remains into a garbage bag. He set the bag beside the pool and then used a garden hose to wash the blood, piss and shit to a drain at the deep end.

Ryan grabbed the trash bag and left the covered pool arena.

Twelve

Madison watched from the window. She saw Ducky leave the pool house first, then Chance strolled out with something cradled in his arms. She couldn't tell what it was. It glistened under the floodlights that illuminated the backyard.

He held it like a baby.

Hunter?

Her mind was not free of the drug's influence, but she was in much better shape now. She had been walking around, cautious for sounds in the hallway. She stayed close to the futon, just in case. She wanted to be laid out on it when they came in. Another dose of whatever they'd given her and she would be out of it for hours.

There was no telling where she was, where the house was located. Outside the window she could see the faint shape of hills, which indicated that they were either near one of the many canyons throughout San Diego County or somewhere in the east county. If she could escape, all she would have to do was find a neighbor, but what if there weren't any neighbors close by?

She'd tried the door. It was locked, as she expected. Had it been open, what would she have done? There was no way to tell what was on the other side and how many people were in the house.

And what the fuck are they doing here?

The clicking sound of the lock came out of nowhere. As the door opened, Madison leapt onto the futon, but she wasn't quick enough. As Ducky entered the room she did her best to put on a dazed look, but her breasts were jiggling from her quick movements, which was a dead giveaway that she wasn't as sedate as she hoped to convey.

Ducky, a cool stride in his gait, stopped and tilted his head, eyes reduced to questioning slits. He shook his head.

"My my, you've recovered from the drugs, haven't you?" he kept shaking his head as a smile surfaced. "I was sure Ryan and Chance would have given you another dose. Did you fool them?"

Madison remained still, her face slack, feeling more and more like a fool.

"Cut it out, sweetie. It's not a good look for you."

Madison stared into his eyes, wondering how fast he was. Could she get past him and lock the door from the outside? What then? Would she be able to get away? Would she be able to find Hunter? Would the other men find her?

Ducky's smile dropped, his face twisting into something evil.

"Drop it," he said. "Enough games. I'll just give you another stab with some good shit. Maybe morphine. Or how about that shit that killed Michael Jackson and Whitney Houston. That shit knocks people the fuck out. You wouldn't stand a chance if I gave you that stuff. You might not even live through it."

People in books and movies plead for their lives, but what did they do in the real world? Madison wasn't going to plead with this fucking monster. That's what he wanted. She could see it in his eyes. The last thing Madison wanted was to give this fuck what he wanted.

She decided to continue playing the part of a drugged-out woman.

Ducky stepped closer and kicked Madison's leg with his shiny designer shoe. "Cut the shit!"

The kick hurt, but Madison remained silent, stoic, dead to the world.

"What, do you think I'm going to rape you?" Ducky shook his head. "I'm not a sick fuck. I would never force myself on a woman."

Ducky looked out the window at the pool house arena, eyes squinted, head tilted a bit.

Madison harnessed her inner strength. There was no way to tell if this was the right time to make her move, but there was something about the look on his face, as if he was thinking deeply about what he was to do with her. Even if she didn't make it out of the room, at least she tried.

But, just as Madison shifted to pounce off the futon, Ducky spun around with a look on his face like madness incarnate. He open-hand whacked her in the face. Not so much a slap, but a swift palm to her temple. The blow was heavy, calculated, brutal. Madison went down hard, smacking the floor face first.

Ducky spoke low and stern. "Don't fuck with me."

As he stepped over the unconscious woman, Ducky's face went into a serious grimace that made his lips pout like a petulant child who hasn't been given what he wanted.

She'd pissed herself. Maybe even shit herself, but Ducky wasn't about to check. He hadn't thought about bathroom breaks when he decided to acquire this particular method of feeding the babies.

Kneeling down, Ducky rolled Madison's body to her back. She only wore her pants. Her shirt was probably still on the garage floor. She had one purpose. One job. To feed. That was it. Tilting his head, Ducky looked down at Madison, and then it was as if the answer to his musings came to him in a sudden rush. He lifted his foot and brought down the heel of his designer shoe right on Madison's left kneecap. The force was enough to dislocate the knee.

Madison came out of unconsciousness with a deep gasp of air and then a scream. Her eyes shot open wide, pained. She reached her hand toward the affected knee. Ducky's foot came down on her other kneecap. Her face contorted and reddened, her scream so shrill it was lost somewhere in her throat.

Madison was out. Her legs were twisted at the knees, like a broken doll.

"Try getting out of here again. I dare you."

Ducky left the room, locking the door behind him.

Thirteen

Ducky made it to the pool house arena just as the second match was to begin.

"Where were you?" Ryan asked, eyeing Ducky contemptuously.

Ducky smoothed out his clothes like some kind of gentleman that he wasn't.

"Don't worry about it," he said. "Had something to take care of. Maybe try morphine next time."

The words were spit at Ryan like cryptic accusations.

Ducky snickered. "Do you have something to say, Ryan?"

Ryan clenched his jaw, the muscles flexing, and then shook his head.

"Then let the second match begin," Ducky said.

Ducky stepped to the edge of the pool and looked down at two babies sitting there on their behinds. One of the babies, the one with a B tattooed on its forehead, was larger than the other. Its arms and legs were chubby, but not like a normal baby. It was almost as if the infant had muscles. Its head was oblong and speckled with nubs like tiny horns threatened to poke through. Casualties of previous fights. Scars decorated the little body in zags of puffy, inflamed tissue. The baby sat there like a prize fighter punch-drunk in the ring.

The other baby was fresh-faced and agile, moving around with honest curiosity and a smile to boot. It had no idea what was about to happen. This baby was fascinated by life itself, the way a curious baby should be. It looked up, noticing Ducky looking down, and it smiled, oblivious to the threats that were all around.

"In this match we have the returning champ, the mean machine herself, scarred, bruised and battered, but always victorious, Barbarella!"

There was a mild response from the diminutive gathering, mostly from those who had seen Barbarella fight before.

Ducky went on. "Opposing Barbarella is a fresh face on the baby fights scene, but don't sleep on him. He might look like innocence on all fours, but just you wait. One taste of that sweet angel dust injection and this baby will turn into . . . KILLING MACHINE!"

Mild response from the attendees. Chuckles and quips. Ducky's face tightened up. He looked over his shoulder at Ryan and gave a nod, indicating that it was time to drug the babies. Ryan nodded back.

The fights were always a success in the end, but Ducky rarely got the response he desired while announcing the matches. Though his crowds were small, he would have appreciated more enthusiasm. In his mind he saw large crowds that cheered like at a wrestling or boxing match. He saw himself as the Ed McMahan of baby fights, but what he got was a lackluster smattering of wise cracks, as if these rich fucks could do better.

Ducky knelt down as Ryan descended into the pool. He said, "More this time."

Ryan paused, looked up. "More?"

Ducky nodded.

"You sure?"

Ducky nodded. "Give 'em a show."

"You're sure?"

"Are you questioning my authority?"

"No, it's just—"

"It's just nothing. Do what I say. Higher dose. Let's get them riled the fuck up."

Theresa chimed in. "Just how much of that can you give them before they overdose?"

Ducky stood, tried to conceal his irritation at the spectacle this match was becoming. "We've run many tests, and have been doing these fights for well over a year. It's all very scientific. These are micro doses, based on the weight of the children. A little more than what our calculations call for isn't going to hurt, but should make for an even livelier match."

Ryan dosed the babies. They began crying from the pinch of the needle. Everyone watched in awe, sipping cocktails and smiling in anticipation.

Except for Chance, who didn't care to watch the matches, but was forced to.

At one time he enjoyed them. He was just as much a spectator as the people who paid the absurd entry fee. Now, he sat in the corner with a paper and a list, making notes as certain milestones were achieved during each fight. He noted which baby threw the first punch, which one drew first blood, which one took the first bite. He was the one who made note of all the items that were being bet on.

He wished he didn't have to watch the fights. He wished he could get out of this lifestyle. He wished he'd never become involved with Ducky's psycho entrepreneurship in the first place. It had been fun, at first. The exhilaration Chance felt when they began doping up babies with speed and watching them battle it out was unlike anything he'd ever experienced in his life. But after so many fights he'd begun to realize that he was involved in something very, very bad. Something he couldn't get out of. He'd done very bad things, all at Ducky's instruction, and though in the beginning he was into it all, he now loathed every aspect of his life. He felt tethered to Ducky, and there was no way out. Ducky had enough on Chance to have him put away for life.

Yes, Chance had stuff on Ducky too, but the operation was like dominoes. When one fell, the others would follow. There was no way out. Not unless Ducky wanted out. As the days passed and Chance had to kidnap babies, and now women, he felt more and more of his soul dying. He was a mere husk. A zombie. With every match he watched, every dead baby, every night of absurd bloodsport, he died a little bit more. Chance wanted out, and there was no escape.

Well, almost no escape.

The babies stopped crying, their voices taking on a hissing, guttural tone like wild animals. Chance sprung to attention, prepared with his pen to jot down notes.

Killing Machine, the fresh-faced babe, rolled around the pool floor quivering and bouncing like bacon in a screaming hot pan. Barbarella shook, but remained in place. Her chubby little hands were held out, fingers splayed. Her eyes got wider and wider as she became flushed, her breathing accelerating into something on the verge of hyperventilation. She then puked, milky substance running down her chin. She puked again and again, now awash in Madison's milk. She puked until there was nothing left, until she was dry heaving like a cat trying to cough up a hairball.

Killing Machine pounded his arms and legs in the concrete bottom of the pool, making agonized cries as tears wet his face from eyes that seemed to be pressurized, popping out like something on a Halloween mask. He rolled again, as if unsure what to do to fend off the feeling his little body was experiencing. He rolled into Barbarella and the fight began.

As Killing Machine bumped into her, she growled and smacked him across the face.

Chance noted that Barbarella made the first move.

Killing Machine didn't take the attack lightly. He scrambled like he was on fire, kicking and hitting Barabrella, but not getting any force behind his maneuvers with his position lying on his side. Barbarella retreated, but only far enough to get away from the onslaught of tiny hands and feet. She then got up on her legs and took a couple crooked steps forward, dropping onto Killing Machine with a pile drive, smashing his head into the concrete.

Killing machine scrambled frantically, grabbing and throwing the girth of Barbarella off of himself. At this, the crowd gasped.

Chance jotted notes. His breathing increased. He wanted to get out of there. Just run. He could live his life as a fugitive. He could run off to Mexico. He'd lay low for a while. Ducky wouldn't go to the authorities, he was sure of that, but he would probably hire a hit man. No loose ends. That's what Ducky always said.

No loose ends.

Sometimes Chance fantasized about killing Ducky. He'd be on the run no matter what. Were Ducky to die, and the authorities checked his house, there would be mountains of evidence tying Chance to the Baby Fights. He would be put on the most wanted list for sure. Ryan would as well. One way or another, if he were to leave he would be running from the law or a hit man. The more he thought about it like that, the more he realized his life was over. He was truly fucked. No more than Ducky's slave.

The crowd gasped and then cheered, snapping Chance out of his daydreams of killing Ducky. He focused on the babies in the empty pool, but had no idea what just happened to cause such a reaction. Possibly something that he needed to note for the bets? This was something that caused a great deal of stress for Chance. Were he to fuck up on the bets, the patrons would become angry, which in turn would cause Ducky to become infuriated. Ducky would have to settle up with his clients, thus losing money. Later, once everyone was gone, Ducky would punish Chance.

Chance just hoped he didn't fuck up, because he'd had about as much of Ducky's punishments as he could handle.

BABY FIGHTS

The fight continued. Barbarella grabbed Killing Machine's arm and clenched her hand, breaking the bones in his wrist. The baby screamed and waved its arm, the hand flopping around. The look on his face was part terror, part anger, and just a touch of fascination. Killing Machine then used the floppy hand like a mace and swung it at Barbarella repeatedly, swatting her in the face. The broken bones ripped through the flesh around Killing Machine's wrist, blood weeping from the fresh wounds. Barbarella reached out and grasped the floppy hand, yanking. The flesh ripped and his hand came free, connected only by stretchy muscle, ligaments, and veins that were rupturing, squirting blood that mixed with the sheen of mother's milk on Barbarella's body.

The patrons watched in silence, cringing and gasping, but never looking away, fascinated with the vile spectacle they'd paid to witness.

The torn stump hardly slowed Killing Machine, who was quickly living up to his moniker. He crawled across the concrete, using his stub like a pirate uses a wooden leg. Barbarella reared back and hissed defensively like some kind of battered, fleshy lizard. She then thwacked Killing Machine a few good times, right on the head, and hard. Killing Machine, having none of that, jabbed at her with his damaged arm, puncturing Barbarella's stomach with the sharp edge of broken bone that protruded from his wrist. The puncture erupted in blood that spilled down her legs. She cried, but only for a few seconds before her cries turned to screams.

Barbarella went into a full-blown panic. A tantrum of the highest order. Kicking and punching and going for the soft spots. Realizing that he had an advantage—or maybe finding the act fun—Killing Machine used the bloody length of sharp bone and jabbed at Barbarella over and over. He gutted her, punctured her little arms and legs, put abrasions all over her face and head until he hit pay dirt and landed a jab right in her left eye.

Finally Barbarella collapsed. As she lay there bleeding out, Killing Machine took on the role he'd been given, slamming the bony stub into her body again and again, seeming to take some kind of sick joy in puncturing her flesh. He jabbed out both eyes, pushing his tiny arm into the sockets as far as it would go, as if trying to tickle her brain. He tore at her gut, opening her belly and spilling her entrails.

The crowd watched, murmuring to themselves, shocked but unable take their eyes off of the spectacle.

Killing Machine calmed, looking down at the torn corpse before him. They were both awash in blood, so much blood. Then Killing Machine lifted his stub of an arm and waved it around. The animalistic sounds he made while further destroying her corpse were now replaced with the wails and cries of a normal baby, eyes scrunched as tears rinsed lines down his chubby, bloody face.

Ducky stood there, mouth agape, shaking his head. "Oh my, and here I thought I'd seen it all." He looked over his shoulder at Chance. "Did you get all that?" And then tilted his head. "Chance? What the fuck are you doing?"

Chance had his head bowed on the little desk he sat at, like a kid sleeping on their desk in school. His body quivered as he sobbed.

Ducky sighed. "What the fuck are you doing, Chance?"

Chance lifted his head, face red, a sheen of tears glossing over his cheeks. He shook his head. "I can't take it anymore." Chance took in gasping breaths like a child in a tantrum. He shook his head again. "I can't watch this shit. I can't."

"Well, I hope you took notes on the bets. You have one job to do, just one job—"

"My ass! I have all kinds of jobs here. Jobs I don't want to do." Chance stood. "I can't take this anymore. I can't do this shit!"

Ducky remained calm. "Now, Chance, this is something we should talk about after our guests have left, don't you think?"

The guests looked around uneasy. They knew what they had witnessed was something that could land them all in prison for the rest of their lives. If things got out of hand, if the authorities were called, things could get ugly real quick. Ducky noticed this look on his guests' faces.

"You know, Chance, you're startling our guests." Ducky shook his head, taking a step forward, toward Chance. "That really isn't a smart thing for you to do. You see, we're all connected to this. We're all in this together. Your behavior right now, well, it could cause some people to think about ways to get rid of you."

Ducky glanced at the guests, glad to see that a few of them nodded.

"What we do here," Ducky went on, "is not something that you can merely quit or be fired from. You know that, right?"

Chance nodded. Tears dripped off his face. "But I can't take it anymore."

Chance revealed that he was holding a syringe. Ducky paused. Chance's eyes darted from each of the customers, to Ryan, to Ducky. He then plunged the needle into his flesh, right into the vein. Ducky leapt forward, but he was too late. Chance depressed the plunger, injecting himself with a fat load of drugs.

"What was that?" Ducky asked.

Chance's face became beet red almost immediately, sweat beading on his brow and upper lip.

"What do you think?" Chance said.

"You fucking moron."

Veins bulged around Chance's neck. His eyes darted around his head, opening and closing rapidly.

"Everyone," Ducky said, "I advise you leave the premises immediately. I will contact all of you with full refunds for these matches." Ducky kept his eyes on Chance as he spoke. "You are not safe here, not now that this dumb motherfucker shot himself up with a monster dose of angel dust. He's about to turn into a raging monster."

Ducky's eyes never left Chance's as he said, "Ryan, take care of Killing Machine. Do whatever you have to do. If he's too badly hurt, kill him. I don't give a shit."

Ryan nodded. "On it."

Chance shifted his attention to Ryan. Chance's breathing accelerated, his chest heaving in and out.

"Over here!" Ducky said.

Chance pivoted back to face Ducky as the patrons quickly fled the pool house.

"What you did," Ducky said, "was fucking stupid, and I don't mind saying that." Ducky held out his right hand and patted his hip. "I'm armed, you fucking animal."

Chance shook his head. "You won't use it." His breathing accelerated, chest heaving more and more. "You don't want to attract attention."

"The hell I won't use it. I'll use it to save my life."

"Oh yeah?" Chance took a step forward.

Ryan tensed, the sedated form of Killing Machine dangling in his arms like a sack of flour.

Ducky remained in position without so much as a flinch, eyes trained on Chance. "Don't even think about it. Now you've got a head full of drugs. You're temporarily psychotic."

"Shoot me. Go ahead."

"You think you'll just walk away from it. Like the guy who slid down the telephone pole naked. Are you that high? Do you want to deal with those consequences?"

Ryan left the pool house with Killing Machine in hand. Barbarella's tiny body lay on the floor of the pool in a puddle of darkening blood.

Chance's breathing accelerated more and more, his body heaving. Sweat poured down his face like a drip system in a garden, soaking his shirt. His skin reddened, eyes bulging, veins popping like they were having trouble accommodating his blood pressure.

Finally, Ducky began to show signs of fear, present in his eyes, which darted around as if seeking out the best method of escape.

Chance's breathing turned to quick, psychotic gasps of air.

Ducky said, "Holy fuck! That baby's still alive!"

Chance turned to look into the pool. In that moment, Ducky ran to the door and slipped out of the pool house. On the other side, he closed the door and hit the "lock" insignia on the keypad deadbolt he'd installed so that no one would be able to enter the arena without the code, of which only he knew. The deadbolt slid into place only a moment before Chance began slamming his fists on the door with such power it seemed as if a giant had been locked in there.

Ducky ran to the pool house where Ryan typically went after a fight to deposit the remains in the deep freezer.

Turns out Ducky hadn't seen it all, and this night was filled with even wilder surprises than Chance's betrayal.

Fourteen

Madison woke with pain. Her legs were numb, and yet they felt as if they were on fire. It took her brain a few minutes to remember what had happened, where she was, and why she couldn't move her legs.

Her bleary vision coalesced after blinking several times, revealing that she was in a room, *the* room where that evil son of a bitch had stomped on her knees.

Looking down at the state of her legs, Madison gasped, sucking air through clenched teeth. Her knees were contorted, the kneecaps twisted like nubs buried in flesh-colored clay that had been pushed out of whack. Purplish bruising was beginning to set in. Once she saw the damage, she felt the pain through the numbness and tingling. Madison tried moving her legs, gasping as jolts of pain shot up her thighs.

As she sat there thinking about how bad things had gotten, she became fully aware that if she didn't do something to remove herself from this situation, she would die there, and it wouldn't be a quick death. That asshole Ducky would kick her and beat her and force her to breastfeed random babies until she couldn't move. Her nipples were already sore and getting chapped. At the rate they were using her breasts as a milk bar she'd be lucky if her nipples didn't crack and bleed before too long.

In the time that Madison had been trapped in the room, before her kneecap stomp fest and during lucid moments before passing out again, she'd thought about what kind of operation was going on in the house. She figured they were selling babies on the black market, using this place to house them.

She'd thought about how she would go through the house and find Hunter, but those hopes were drifting further and further away. The primal instinct of survival was strong. She would die finding Hunter, but none of that could happen if she couldn't even get out of the damn room.

Using her upper body and hips, Madison crawled across the floor to the second door in the room, assuming the door Ducky and his goons used was locked. This second door opened freely, leading into a bathroom. A Jack and Jill bathroom by the looks of the door directly across from the one she opened.

Madison crawled in, finding it easier to maneuver her body than she'd anticipated. The throbbing in her knees was a distraction, but survival was a goal. Madison was no slouch. She'd had to take on life regardless of what was put in her way, and she always prevailed.

In the bathroom, she opened the lower cabinet of the sink, but only found cleaners and soaps. Nothing she could use. She'd hoped to find drugs. Painkillers. If anything was there, it would be in the medicine cabinet.

But the pain in her legs was such that she couldn't stand. Madison tried and tried again, stabbing pains escalating her thighs and shooting like knives into the lower abdomen. Her feet were numb, as if the circulation had been completely cut off from her knees down. At first there was a pins and needles sensation, but now there was nothing.

Crawling to the next door, Madison reached up and turned the knob, pushing it gently into another room, this one lit with several little night lights. There were cribs all around, with the movements of babies.

Fifteen

As Ducky neared the diminutive pool house, he smelled something awful. He'd gotten whiffs of this smell before, assuming it to be a dead animal by the creek bed down the bluff just past his back fence. He'd smelled dead animals there a lot. It had been a long time since Ducky had been in the pool house. He'd seen Ryan there many times, but he had no desire to busy himself with disposing the refuse of their death matches. They had a good method that Ryan had come up with, deep-freezing the dead babies before incinerating them.

Ducky had always assumed that things were going fine. He had no reason to think otherwise, but as he put his hand on the doorknob, and the smell of death intensified, his stomach dropped.

Ducky opened the door, fully expecting the deep freezer to be broken, and the bodies that had been stored there to be rotting and causing the foul odor. What he found was something he never could have prepared himself for.

BABY FIGHTS

There are moments in life when it feels as if everything comes crashing down like a piano being craned out of a high-rise apartment that is too heavy for the tethers. Ducky should have been able to see the writing on the wall. He should have been able to prepare for this, to stop this from happening.

Ryan stood there with a torch lighter roasting the torn stub where Killing Machine's hand had been ripped off in the ring. The tiny body lay there like a stuffed animal that had lost half its stuffing. The smell of burned flesh overpowered the reek of death momentarily as the human smoke swirled around the grotesque pool house.

Ducky opened his mouth to say something, but the words were caught in his throat. In addition to the mad scene before him was the grisly décor.

"You sick fuck," was all Ducky could say, as if anything could truly be sicker than drugging babies and having them fight to the death.

The room was alight with the glow of strand after strand of Christmas lights, weaved in and around a psychotic tableau of rotting baby carcasses that had been affixed to the walls like some kind of vile art movement. The corpses were in various stages of decomposition, lights connecting each little rotten infant to the next. Some of the older ones had lights shoved into their little bodies, causing them to glow. One baby, indistinguishable as an individual human being at this point, had two red bulbs where its eyes should have been, giving it a creepy crimson death stare.

Ryan stood there, eyes wide, dead baby limp in his arms. The festering wound he tried to cauterize wept burnt blood onto the floor. He had been caught, and he had no idea how to deal with the consequences he clearly knew would be hurled his way.

After several deep breaths, Ducky calmed himself before he did what his instincts told him, which was to throttle Ryan and add him to the macabre collection, and then set the damn pool house on fire.

Instead, Ducky said, "We can fix this." His voice was flat, then became more animated. "But first we have to deal with Chance. He's gone over the edge. He injected himself with freebase. Not a micro dose for the fights, but the real deal."

As if punctuating that statement, there was a loud crashing sound outside that caught both Ducky and Ryan off guard, causing them both to crouch. Ducky stepped out of the death-stinking shack to see Chance rushing into the house. The door to the pool house had been broken open, hanging awkward on the twisted hinges.

"Fuck! The shit's kicking in. He's probably looking for me."

"If—" Ryan's voice was small in the shack, a tepid thing.

Ducky turned. "If what?"

"Are you going to kill me? If you do, please—" Ryan looked at the walls of the shack, at his collection aglow under brilliant lights. "Please leave me here so I can be with my art. With my darlings."

Ducky's face churned into a rictus of disgust. He closed his eyes, shook his head, and left the building.

Sixteen

The room smelled like babies. A soft smell. A delicate smell. But one Madison knew well. She was so immediately reminded of her son that survival, in that instant, had been vanquished from her mind, at least on a solely personal level. In that moment, Madison was sure that Hunter was in there. She just had to find him.

The shock was wearing off, leaving her in a world of pain. Her knees felt like someone had poured molten steel on them. The burn was intense, and they seemed to be seizing up, causing each movement to erupt in waves of agonizing fire. Even thinking about standing caused Madison to shudder.

Crawling across the floor, wincing in agony, she made her way to the first crib, trying to sit as much as possible to take the strain off of her knees. Madison had heard the phrase *mind over matter*, and she liked to believe that, but right about now her mind was being tested, and she was losing the battle.

She could see herself standing, just ignoring the pain and standing. She thought that's what survival was, standing and ignoring the pain, gritting her teeth and hurtling any obstacle for the sake of living, especially when Hunter was involved, but that wasn't the case. The man had broken her legs. No one could walk on broken legs.

It wasn't that the desire to find her son had ever really fled, but that his survival depended on her own survival.

All that changed when she entered the nursery.

Dragging herself to the first crib, Madison looked through the bars on the side. Within she saw something that caused her to recoil. It was a baby, but not exactly what she'd expected. Its face was covered in cuts and sores and bruises like nothing Madison had ever seen before. Not on a baby. This was never supposed to happen to babies.

A jolt of shock hit her when she considered that this might be Hunter, but she could tell it wasn't. This baby had different hair (there were angry looking sores where tufts of the hair had been yanked out), and different eyes. But what were they doing here? Abusing babies? And what for?

She inched her way to the next crib and what she found caused her to break down. It was worse than the NICU, seeing the teeny tiny preemies all hooked up to tubes and machines. These were someone's babies. Somewhere out there were mothers with holes in their hearts for these missing children, and they were terribly abused. Scarred, scraped, and bruised. The face that looked back at Madison through the wooden slatted railing of the next crib was lumpy and bruised so severely the child looked as if it suffered from some kind of disease that left its skin the color of a rotting banana. One eye was swollen shut, the other leaking a pus-like discharge. The look on the baby's face, deep beneath the battered veneer, was blank, as if it had seen too much, had endured too much. It was shell shocked, as they used to say. Severely traumatized into a state of catatonia.

Madison wept, staring at this child, this baby that didn't deserve whatever had happened to it. And what for? That was the question that haunted her more than anything. What the fuck for?

As Madison wept, knees throbbing as if her legs had been dismembered and then dipped in salt, the door to the room opened. She looked up, fearing her discovery and also in such a low place that she felt as of nothing could touch her, not in a way that would shock her any further. What she'd seen in that room killed her soul. At this point, all these freaks could do was torture her body and though that would be painful, her death would bring sweet release from the horrors of this twisted house.

It was the larger man, the bearded man who had seemed more apprehensive than the others. He saw her on the floor and stared at her with eyes that seemed poised to pop out of his face. His skin was red like he'd spent too much time in the sun, and he breathed heavily. His mouth opened as if to say something, and then closed again, this action happening over and over like a fish out of water or some kind of mechanical failure. In his hands were two babies. He set them on the floor, not gingerly, but not too forcefully either.

One of the babies was Hunter.

Everything changed in that moment. Madison had been on the verge of giving up, just lying there on the floor in that room of abused infants and giving the fuck up. And then she saw her baby boy.

The man dashed away down the hall, its dark gloom waiting at the doorway like an exit to some kind of hell. Madison made a move toward Hunter, wincing at the pain in her legs, but she could do it. Unless the bones were broken, she would force herself to stand, just to get out of there with her baby.

"Hunter," she said.

He looked up and his world came alive. The smile on his face was everything to Madison in that moment. It was hurricane force memories from the past year of their life together, all sweeping over with heavy doses of raw emotion. As Hunter crawled across the floor to Mommy, the bearded man, Chance, entered the room again with two more infants clutched in his arms. He put these babies on the floor and closed the door.

When Chance brandished a syringe, Madison cringed.

It wasn't over yet.

Chance breathed in harsh gasps of air, his chest heaving like he was on the verge of hyperventilation. His movements were jerky, but he knew what he was doing, or so it seemed, as he grabbed the first baby and gave it a small dose from the syringe.

Madison watched in horror.

"What are you doing?" she asked, immediately regretting those words.

Chance looked up, his body twitching all over, his movements jerky. He was clearly on something.

"Motherfucker ain't gonna do this shit no more," he said. "No fucking more."

Spittle flew from his mouth as he spoke. The muscles in his face twitched. He looked like a homeless man who'd spent the day yelling at the reapers in his head.

"Let me go." The words were out of Madison's mouth before she could even comprehend what she was saying. They were more instinctual than she ever thought while watching horror films and scoffing at weak women pleading for their lives. She realized in that moment it had nothing to do with being weak. It was survival instinct. It was something to distract the psychopath.

Chance's face twisted into confusion. "I can't. I . . . I can't. Let you go."

"You don't want to do this. I can see that."

Chance gritted his teeth and growled. "Like fire in my veins!"

He grabbed another baby and injected it. Then another.

Madison prepared herself as Chance got closer.

Seventeen

Ducky entered the house yelling for Chance.

"You fucking animal, where are you?"

No response.

"Fine," Ducky said as he ascended the stairs. "I'll find you myself, you rotten piece of shit. You'll be sorry. You're gonna pay for this dearly, you hear me?"

Nothing.

Chance had been easy to control. He was a born follower, the type of person Ducky thrived around. Ducky hadn't considered Chance a threat, he and Ryan both being such losers. Ducky figured guys like them needed leaders. Turned out they needed more than that, considering what Ryan had been doing in his spare time. Now it appeared Chance had a heart. Who would have known? They'd all done horrible things, but the more Ducky pondered why this was happening and how it started, the more he realized Chance had been less and less involved. He'd been there at every match, taking notes, but not taking pleasure in the violence like Ducky and Ryan always had, and continued to do.

"Chance! Where the fuck are you?" Ducky hollered from the upstairs hall.

There were sounds from within nursery number one, the recovery unit where battle scarred babies were treated to fight another day.

The door to nursery number one opened. Ducky didn't have time to respond before a pair of beefy hands grabbed him. He struggled, but the grip was inhuman, yanking Ducky into the room. Flung to the floor, Ducky scrambled to get upright and make sense of the assault when he caught a glimpse of Chance on the hallway side of the door, closing and locking it from the outside.

A choir of hissing erupted around Ducky as if he'd been dropped into a snake den like in *Raiders of the Lost Ark*, only these weren't snakes. They were babies hopped up on angel dust.

Ducky swatted the first one away with a swift palm to its chubby face, but the drugs were coursing through their little bodies like battery acid. They were agitated and ornery. The smack hardly did anything, and before Ducky could think, two more drug-crazed babies were on him.

Fending off one or two was no problem, but there were too many. They kicked and threw punches that were far stronger than any little baby fist had any right to be. They clamped onto his flesh with their gums like pit bulls, tearing muscle without breaking the flesh.

Ducky screamed and flailed, but he couldn't get them off.

Their eyes were wild, faces contorted. The same looks he'd seen in the pool house ring. They'd been dosed, and the freebase was strong in their veins. Ducky recognized some of them from previous fights. He recognized the healing wounds. The swollen eyes, the cauliflowered ears, their bodies lumpy with swollen, welted flesh.

As the babies went for Ducky's soft spots, he swatted them away, conscious of their efforts, but he was no match. Their numbers were too great. He felt a rip at his side, and then an explosion of pain, hot and searing like someone pouring vinegar on an open wound. Ducky was unable to see down, considering there were two babies on his head, trying to poke his eyes out. One stuck her finger in his ear and pushed with superhuman strength, rupturing his eardrum. Ducky let out a howl and tried to swat the hand away when another set of tiny digits caught his hand and bent several of his fingers backward, the bones cracking. Ducky let out another pained screech, which seemed to excite them.

They became frenzied, making garbled growling noises as they searched for the soft spots in Ducky's body that could be penetrated. He felt something at his side, a small hand pushing through the source of pain that he could not see. He was sure one of them had started playing with his guts. He'd heard of men in war being blasted and holding their insides in while seeking medical help, but how long could someone survive like that?

Finally a pair of eager digits like little plump breakfast sausages found his right eye and pushed not-so-gently, rupturing the orb, spilling blood and ocular fluid down Ducky's face like the contents of a rotten egg. Ducky's screams reached new heights. He scrambled around, but was unable to see where he was going, eventually collapsing to the ground where the little bastards had the advantage.

When Ducky next screamed, hands grabbed the sides of his cheeks and yanked, ripping the flesh to expose his gums and molars, shiny with dental work, all awash in blood. Teeth were yanked and violently plucked out, their crude extraction met with absurd giggles. One of them took a tooth and jammed the root end back into his jaw, causing something like an electric surge through Ducky's bloody mouth.

As Ducky lost the fight of his life to a mob of drug-fueled babies, he saw a figure rise from the corner of the room.

Eighteen

Madison had watched the crazed bearded man inject the babies with something. She'd thought it was something to euthanize them, but she was terribly mistaken. The drug had the exact opposite effect, causing them to become wild beasts.

The man approached her, but she couldn't defend herself as he gave her the same injection. At the moment he administered the drug, she'd still thought it would kill her, and she had come to terms with the fact that she was going to die. In that moment, those were easy terms to accept, considering what she had been through and what she assumed a prolonged stay in that house would entail.

Madison had been cradling Hunter when the man grabbed her baby's arm. She yanked Hunter away from him, but he was forceful. Maternal instinct told her to protect her baby. She had then seen the look in his eyes, the crazed look like he would snap and do something awful to Hunter in retaliation. In that instant, while she thought the drug would sedate and kill her, she realized Hunter would have been

BABY FIGHTS

alone in the house, away from her, and who knew what would happen to him there. It was better they both die together.

It was then that she gave up the struggle and allowed Chance to dose Hunter as he had the others.

After the babies turned into writhing masses like upset maggots, Madison realized that the drug was not what she'd assumed. Her skin became hot and she felt a surge of adrenaline like nothing she'd ever felt before. In those moments after he injected her, she felt as if she could run across the room and back quicker than the blink of an eye, and there was some kind of weird urge to do so. Her movements became jerky, as if she were moving faster than the speed of time itself.

Hunter had become as agitated as the other babies, many of them beginning to cry, and others making weird grunting noises like primitives celebrating a successful hunt.

Madison had seen something in Hunter's eyes. She'd grabbed him, and he swatted at her, hard. He had more strength than he should have, and he seemed angry for some reason.

Madison herself was feeling out of sorts. Urges taunted her mind like waves of electricity that snapped in her brain with thoughts of destruction. Nonsensical thoughts. Madison tried her best to ignore the urges as she'd used a blanket to tightly swaddle Hunter, pinning his arms and legs into the burrito-like fold. All the while the other babies, all of whom had been pulled from their cribs and placed on the floor, became more and more agitated.

Things happened fast. The babies were like little monsters when Ducky was thrust into the room. It was like something from a zombie movie, the way the little bodies threw themselves at Ducky, grabbing his arms and legs and pulling at him. Biting with gummed jaws that had the snap of little gators and crocodiles. They garbled and screeched as they took out their burning drug-fueled mania on the man who was the cause for all of this madness.

Madison felt it too. The urge. The burning inside. Hunter squirmed around in her grasp like an oversized earthworm exposed to the sun. Watching the mayhem, Madison felt a tinge of fear, though she somehow knew that the violent babies wouldn't turn on her. It was almost as if being dosed at the same time like that put them into some collective psychosis.

Rising from her position in the corner of the Room (the drug eliminated, for now, the pain in her knees), Madison staggered on contorted legs toward the door as the vicious babies continued their savage act of violence. Madison wasn't one for revenge, but she couldn't help feeling like the men who were doing all of this deserved what they got. As she passed by Ducky, his remaining eye pleading, she felt an urge to join the babies. It swept over her like fire in her veins, rising from her feet to her head where the sensation sat like smoldering embers in a mind that was completely twisted on whatever concoction had been injected into her bloodstream.

Pausing, Madison stared down at Ducky as he screamed and yelled, blood erupting from torn flesh the babies penetrated with eager fingers. One baby played with the guts that had been pulled from the side of his stomach. Another chewed his torn throat, its cherub face red and dripping. And yet another had managed to pull down his pants, extracting his cock and using it like a teething device, squishing the flesh-tube between soft gums.

Madison clenched her teeth as she held back the strong urge to join them. The smell of his blood rose around her like a copper vapor, a sickening odor that threatened a vomit reaction. Madison threw up in her mouth and spit the bile in Ducky's face before walking out of the room with her precious squirming baby clasped tight in her arms.

The house was silent outside of the massacre taking place in the nursery. Madison made her way downstairs, but was disorientated. She hadn't known the layout of the house in the first place, having been carted off to one of the upstairs rooms right from the garage. On top of that, her mind was on fire. Her blood felt like lava. The drugs were coursing through her veins in a way she was not prepared for. It was like nothing she'd ever experienced in her life, and she could understand why the infants upstairs had the reaction they'd exhibited. Given a few more minutes and she would have torn apart the first person she saw, just to try and release some of this pressure building up inside of her.

But Madison decided on something else rather than violence, her not being the violent type, even though, at that moment, violence seemed like a superb idea. She saw, through a set of large bay windows, the yard. Front yard, backyard, she had no idea. It was outside, and that was what she wanted most of all. Get into the cool night air and stop this burning that seemed to be emanating from within her body.

The door was left open. Madison exited the house into the cool air of night. She was in the backyard. Everything was quiet. After she took a moment to catch her breath, to calm some despite how amped up the drugs made her feel, she noticed a strange glow from an out building. It looked like a little pool house or shed.

Hunter cried and squirmed, but he was manageable. He would be okay, Madison would be sure of that.

The compulsion to investigate the strange light caused Madison's legs to move her in that direction before she'd even made her mind up about what to do. The closer she got, the more she realized that she should turn and flee, but the more things became clear, the more her legs moved her forward.

First, she saw the bloody footprints, then she got a glimpse through the door of what was inside the shed. Just a quick look before a voice to her left caught her attention. Inside the shed were dead babies hanging from the walls and entangled with Christmas lights. Hanging there, gently swaying, was one of the men who had abducted her. The noose was fashioned from a heavy-duty strand of lights that glowed around his neck. He'd been disemboweled, the raw cavity of his gut filled with a tangle of red lights that were set to flicker and glow, casting a bizarre effect like animated intestines.

The moaning sound issued again from Madison's left. She turned and, thanks to the glow of the moon and floodlights, saw where the bloody footprints led. The bearded man was on the other side of a black iron fence. He'd jumped and caught his jaw on one of those decorative spikes, the black iron entering from below and protruding right through his lower jaw and out of his mouth, causing him to be stuck there in what looked like a terribly painful manner, though he had enough freebase in his bloodstream to help dull the pain.

He tried to speak words, but all that came out was a garbled wet mess of syllables. In his frustration, he made jerky movements, but could not free himself. Blood glistened in the moonlight, trailing down his bare chest. At some point he'd removed all of his clothes, and Madison could understand why. She was burning up, but still had a modicum of her senses, enough so to realize that she needed to get the hell out of there and call the police.

She turned to leave, Hunter held tight. She kissed him on the head, feeling the warmth radiating from his little body. Behind her, Chance screamed and wailed, the iron fence rattling beneath his pinned girth.

Just as Madison made it to a gate that led out to the front yard, Chance screamed loud enough to alert neighbors. Madison turned and looked, but he wasn't there. All that was left, visible under the heavy glow of floodlights, was his bloody jaw hanging by a rope of meat.

Running up the street with Hunter clutched tight, Madison felt comforted by the porch lights that turned on as she screamed and screamed and screamed.

About The Author

Robert Essig is the author of over fifteen books such as *Broth House*, *Tweaker Creatures*, *Mojave Mud Caves*, and *Death Obsessed*. He has published over 150 short stories, some of them collected in *Shallow Graves* (with Jack Bantry), and the forthcoming *Infected Voices*, which has been serialized on Godless.com. He had edited three small press anthologies, one of which, *Chew On This!*, was nominated for a Splatterpunk Award. Robert was born and raised in San Diego, and now lives with his family in east Tennessee.

Subscribe to Robert's newsletter for free:

robertessig.substack.com
Purchase signed copies of Robert's books at:

ressighorror.bigcartel.com

Also By Robert Essig

At Broth House our soups are made from only the finest fresh ingredients, sourced locally through donations. Our charitable restaurant believes that even the homeless and downtrodden deserve a good meal.

A gourmet meal. The meats are sourced locally too. Made from only the best stock. Everyone deserves a warm meal in their belly.

Bon appetit!

Brad and Jeffery are having the night of their lives when tragedy strikes like a slaughtering hammer to a cow's skull. After a fatal meeting with the Butter Boys, they will never be the same.

"Robert Essig excels at creating an ominous atmosphere leading to a sense of impending doom. He allows his audience to grasp a well written storyline before feeding a heaping spoonful of humiliation, torture and death." – Horror Bookworm Reviews

A group of young Spring Breakers headed for Lake Havasu take a sudden detour in the middle of the Mojave Desert. It will be a quick stop, he said. It won't take long, he said. It's hot. Over 100 degrees, and no one really wants to meddle around some sweaty desert caves a mile off the highway. Then something goes wrong and no one knows what to do. Needles, California, a town in regression, home of semi-retired truck driver Big Vic. He's made a lot of mistakes in life and has vowed to make a change, starting by spending more time his adult daughter who has suddenly gone missing. Is it drugs, a kidnapping, murder? His investigation teams him up with an unlikely ally and he finds that tapping into his rough and tumble past is the only way to get answers. In the desert of Southern California is something of a phenomenon. Tucked away from passersby on Interstate 40 and widely unknown, a series of tunnels crisscross through the mountains, but they're not mine shafts or caverns. They're not teaming with bats and stalagmites. These tunnels are deliberate. Festering with something ferocious, something deadly. Something evil.

What lurks within the Mojave Mud Caves?

MONSTERS COME OUT

Veronica Hensley's life took a massive detour the day a murderous clown showed up on her doorstep. That's the day the world changed forever, the day half of the human population spontaneously mutated. The day the monsters came out. It didn't take long for society to crumble, all spurred on by fear mongering media outlets and vigilante groups run amok.

The monstrous beings are deemed to be dangerous, and many of them are, but others are kind and gentle and being ostracized for no reason other than a change in appearance that they have no control over.

Veronica, a freelance investigative reporter, cannot stand to see what is happening to the world around her, and steps in to help the innocent mutations as hateful psychos and the evil fringes of the law wreck havoc on the crumbling city of San Diego, California.

As sides are chosen and power struggles create divides, the future of society as we know it hangs in the balance. Questions of good and evil are answered at the hands of the murderous, both man and monster.

Printed in Great Britain
by Amazon